Rich and Poor

Rich and Poor
Jacob Wren

BookThug
Department of Narrative Studies
Toronto, 2016

FIRST EDITION

Cover painting *Total Fortune Spray* by John McConville. Used with permission.

The production of this book was made possible through the generous assistance of the Canada Council for the Arts and the Ontario Arts Council. BookThug also acknowledges the support of the Government of Canada through the Canada Book Fund and the Government of Ontario through the Ontario Book Publishing Tax Credit and the Ontario Book Fund.

LIBRARY AND ARCHIVES CANADA CATALOGUING IN PUBLICATION

Wren, Jacob, author
    Rich and poor / Jacob Wren.

Issued in print and electronic formats.
paperback: ISBN 978-1-77166-238-3
html: ISBN 978-1-77166-239-0
pdf: ISBN 978-1-77166-240-6
mobi: ISBN 978-1-77166-241-3

    I. Title.

PS8595.R454R53 2016   C813'.54   C2016-900593-3 | C2016-900594-1

PRINTED IN CANADA

A **bundled** eBook edition is available
with the purchase of this print book.

CLEARLY PRINT YOUR NAME ABOVE IN UPPER CASE

Instructions to claim your eBook edition:
1. Download the Shelfie app for Android or iOS
2. Write your name in **UPPER CASE** above
3. Use the Shelfie app to submit a photo
4. Download your eBook to any device

Part 1

1.

There is the expression: you catch more flies with honey than you do with poison. But I have realized this is only partly true. Because unless your goal is to breed flies, you also need at least a little bit of poison to finish them off. Looking back on my life I now wonder: what was the honey and what was the poison? How often did I confuse the two and with what results? The standard rags-to-riches story is a tepid, sugary cliché, and the ways I have often used it to charm and increase my opportunities in life, and how I will continue to do so here, is one of the many poisons that harms me daily to a similar degree as I have damaged the many who have stumbled into my path. To make yourself a legend you tell your story one way, and to make yourself a martyr you tell it differently, with different emphasis. Both ways are of course corrupt but the results differ. I've never been good at introducing myself, one reason that I prefer everyone already know who I am before I arrive. It was never my intention to write a memoir. I've never understood why memoirs are so popular these days.

The Persian philosopher Tusi (AD 1201–1274) writes: "If men were equal, they would all perish." We need differences between rich and poor, he insisted, just as we need differences between farmers and carpenters. I wasn't born rich. It took me twenty years of panache and gradual calculation to build my fortune. And if I had children, which I do not, and if like me they had not been born rich, which is rather unlikely, it is even more unlikely they would be able to repeat my success. The world no longer contains such opportunities, and this generalized lack of opportunity is a condition me and my kind had some small part in creating. Or not. Perhaps we only rode the waves of our time, and, if none of us had been born, others would have done the same. But it was us and not others. Much like some people are rich and others are poor. We can say that some people are rich because others are poor but it changes nothing. The roulette wheel spins and the numbers that come up are the ones that win. If you were a left-wing activist in Germany in the twenties or thirties there would be little you could do to stop Hitler. And yet it's important to believe there is always something you can do, to lie to yourself a little, because then at least you have a shot. Miracles do happen but they are extremely rare. My situation was not a miracle. Just a great deal of charm and ambition, and being alive in an age when such things were possible. Plus precisely the right degree of luck. But of course, like all of us in these positions, I don't believe in luck. We all believe, like any good asshole, that success is nothing more or less than the result of our genius.

2.
I will kill him. It will solve nothing and help no one, but for me at least, it will bring something to an end. The poor must kill the rich, one at a time, at every opportunity. One man kills another and the message is clear, your wealth is cruel and unnatural. You can put fences, guards and dogs around your home, so you are like a prisoner in your own life, but if you are rich you will live in fear. You will fear your servants. You will look out the window of your limousine and, at every traffic

light, wonder if each and every passerby has a gun and bullet with your name on it. It is only that the killing must be completely random. The victims having nothing in common other than their wealth, the killers nothing in common other than their poverty. The message should be clear: if you are rich you can be killed at any time. The police would arrest millions but there would always be another poor man that could suddenly snap. We would only have to kill ten to start, to strike fear in the hearts of every billionaire in the world. And he will be the first. I will see to it.

On a social level, people have to look after each other, but on an ethical level, each of us has to look after ourselves. If you are a billionaire it is because you have done evil in the world. You have exploited and caused untold misery. You have bent laws and governments to your will. I don't want to shoot him. I want to strangle him with piano wire. I don't want to escape. I want to be caught and explain my idea to the world. I want to be executed. I now have nothing to lose. We will all be forgotten. But if ten of us manage to kill billionaires those ten will be remembered forever. Our poverty will become history. Wealth is impersonal but we will make it personal again.

1.

Violence has always been a last resort. So much is possible without violence, but so much more with just the threat of it, and even more if you occasionally go over the top. I am not a violent man. Therefore I must work with violent men. Violent men I can trust. There are two kinds of violence I have made use of in my work: violence connected to a government and violence that takes place without any government knowledge. Both have their very specific, but separate, strategic dangers. When you can convince the government to do your violence for you the benefits are obvious, but there are also clear pitfalls: the government might lose popularity, be voted out or overthrown, and your business, having been closely associated with that particular government, might have to go as well. This scenario has played out in my professional life several times. However, even if this were to happen, all is not lost, because there is still the possibility to convince the new government to continue working with you. Violence without the use of government is considerably more costly, since all expenses are your own, but what you lose in the form of money you gain in agency and independence.

If all of this sounds too abstract, and perhaps heartless, one would be correct in assuming that I have seen very little violence first-hand. I mention these facts because I believe something similar happens to all of us. You drive your car knowing it is disastrous for the environment, and yet continue to drive anyway. You drive your kids to school, knowing the very car you're driving them in will make their future more environmentally precarious. You read the newspaper and feel the things within it that disturb you are completely disconnected from your daily actions, when they are not. If you dedicated your life to changing just one of them, something might budge. But you don't because you don't feel that strongly about it. You think it is terrible but not so terrible you are ready to drop everything and take action. Myself, I would prefer to run my business without any recourse to violence, but also, I have to admit, I don't feel so strongly about it. And if I were to do so, it would be impossible to remain competitive. Profits would suffer. Like all of us, the assholes, I have a responsibility to my shareholders.

2.

There is of course a reason, an incident, behind my desire to kill him. I was not born poor. I became poor. Not as a direct result of his actions, but more indirectly, through grief. I experienced a grief so severe I could not work, think or exist. This period lasted for about ten years and I remember very little of it. But there is one thing I remember with absolute clarity. During the years of oblivion I stopped reading literature and stopped reading philosophy. I would occasionally read the newspaper but never managed to get very far. The news all seemed too far away. What I did start reading was corporate shareholder reports. By the end of ten years, just before I was evicted, my apartment was packed with them. I would go to business chat sites and post notices asking stockholders to send me their old ones, that I was collecting them, and literally hundreds started arriving in the mail. Clearly the stockholders had no idea what to do with them, were happy to see them go, forests and forests of the stuff. I would read them obsessively, against the text, as if every proudly announced profit concealed an environmental crime or worse. As if they were not documents of enrichment but of destruction. There was a great deal of truth to my analysis, but this activity was unfortunately not good for my mental health. It was a way to drive myself insane with anger and it worked. I spent god knows how many years driving myself mad in precisely this manner and might still be doing so today if I had not been forced to leave the apartment. Sometimes the things that harm us most are also our saviours.

With the eviction at the forefront of my mind, I started piling up the reports in the alleyway behind my building. It took me an entire week to move them all; I couldn't believe how many I had collected or how big the eventual pile was, like a mountain of pure greed. The night before they kicked me out, I set fire to the mountain and watched it burn for five hours. I expected fire trucks and police but none came. I expected the whole city to burn but the flames kept to themselves, much like the neighbours who I suppose decided to mind their own business and not call the police. As I watched, I imagined it was the corporations themselves that were burning: their headquarters, the CEOs, the private security companies hired to protect them. I imagined that for every forest that was clear-cut, one corporate headquarters building burst into flame as if by magic. For every mother forced to watch her infant starve to death on the poverty wages her husband brought in, one CEO would spontaneously combust. I remember that fire. For five hours I fantasized until the last embers turned black at the brink of dawn. That night was the first step of my long journey back to sanity, towards a more coherent worldview, and also the first kernel, the very beginning, of my eventual plan.

1.

Capitalism is not the simple desire to make a profit. Capitalism is the fantasy that growth can continue at a consistent rate indefinitely. When a child is young, it cannot yet imagine being an adult, so it thinks it will keep growing forever. The fantasy that you can grow forever is exhilarating, one of the many aspects that make children seem so alive. We live in fantasy, all of us, all of the time, to a greater or lesser extent.

Business, on the other hand, is the simple desire to make a profit, along with, if you're lucky, a desire to produce something useful in the world. If you are running a business in this day and age, you are of course doing so within the framework of capitalism. Business is the yoke, capitalism the shell. You cannot write a business plan saying: we just want to make enough money to be comfortable and after that we have no particular desire to grow. (Or you can but it would be difficult to find investors.) You need to project annual growth, as much as possible.

When I was young, I could not possibly imagine obtaining wealth. My father never spoke of such things, and I believe he never thought much of them either. He worked every day and took whatever money they gave him. It was enough to get by, most of the time. I would watch my father carefully, full of childish suspicions, thinking (or was I only hoping) that there must be some easier way. Or perhaps I was hoping no such thing. There are so many details we fill in imaginatively when we tell stories from the distant past. My father died when I was still poor, and sometimes, in more reflective moments, I wonder what he would think of all this: the private planes, posh restaurants (where occasionally I spend more in one night than they would have spent in six months), and endless waves of work, meetings and more work.

Allow me to get sentimental for a moment (as if it was possible to stop me). I spent a great deal of time in the hospital with my father in the weeks leading up to his death. He was a quiet man, didn't talk much, as was the fashion for men of his generation. But in the hospital we talked like we'd never talked before. He told me so many things, and what I grew to understand—what I had never understood before—is that he had lived his life afraid. I didn't want to be afraid, and in one of our last quiet moments together I told him so. I was wrong, he told me, carefully explaining, wanting to set the record straight before it was too late. From the outside it might look like fear, might have appeared that time and time again he had backed down, but inside he had always been content, always felt he had remained focused on the things that were important in life: his family, being relaxed, working efficiently and with integrity, enjoying the small pleasures that each day is kind enough to grant us. He seemed pleased to have explained all this and, not wanting to argue with a dying man, I agreed with him, thanked him for his words, told him they were beautiful and true.

But even then I thought he was lying, both to me and to himself, and that he had in fact lived his life in fear. (I still wonder today whether he knew he had failed to convince me or if I had managed to reassure him.) What's more, it was then I realized that in our last intimate talks, by telling him I knew he was a coward, by seeing through him like that, I had somehow gained the upper hand. I was no longer only his child but also something else, someone who had something on him, who had some small power over him, and he was now afraid of me too. Saying what he did, that he had always been content, was just another way of backing down, like he had his entire life. Later that week he died. I cried when the doctor phoned me. In fact I cried a lot, but nonetheless, I was never going to be like that. I was never going to back down.

2.

His book, his autobiography, is in my hands and fuelling my rage. I saw it in the window as I was walking by a bookstore and the coincidence struck me like a hammer. I quickly shoplifted one—there was no way I was giving that bastard more money—and am reading it now, still amongst the early pages.

What strikes me most is his strange mix of pathos and showmanship. He has doubts, endless moments of doubt, but each and every time he overcomes them and finds his way towards doing exactly the most evil thing he can come up with. It is masterful the way he humanizes himself, since we can all relate to having little moments of struggle, only to turn it around, or inside out—always this constant rejection of basic human values in favour of his own endless egotism. He is self-aware, constantly including himself among the avaricious assholes who have created a world that, if he is honest with himself, not even he wants to live in anymore. But at the same time, he is strangely proud of having created this world. For him, it was an act of will.

I read a few pages then violently throw the book across the room, do something else for awhile, or do nothing, before curiosity eventually gets the best of me and begrudgingly, like a chastened slave, I walk across the room to pick it up off the floor and continue reading. Even after twenty pages the book looks like it has been through a meat grinder. I'm throwing it as hard as I possibly can. But after a few days I start to feel stupid and put the book aside. I'm only halfway through but it's enough for now. There's little in the book that would help me get closer to him, but much in it that might help me win his trust once I eventually do.

There are three private security companies he regularly signs contracts with and I have now applied for jobs at all of them. My resumé is only partly forged, so we will have to see how thoroughly they check. I have three chances but, for now, I am only waiting for a phone call. While I wait, I read about security, about bodyguards, about bulletproof jackets and armoured cars. For money I'm washing dishes a few nights a week in whatever place will take me. I work quietly and efficiently, without incident. I don't need much money so work as little as possible. I keep my phone turned on from nine to six, in case I am called in for an interview. Then in the evening keep it turned off. I talk to almost no one and, when I do, keep the topics light, making light-hearted jokes whenever possible. My heart is not light but, for short stretches, I believe I get away with it. I would find all this beyond boring if I was not so focused on a single goal, a goal that will end my freedom but, hopefully, start something much larger. Life without a goal, without a fulcrum, without a single point of intensity around which everything else can swirl, is not worth living. My life, however dull, is.

Three months go by before I get the first interview, and the time allows me to thoroughly prepare. On my way there, I shoplift a second copy of his book to read while I wait. It is a careless risk, since if I was caught my entire plan would be sabotaged. But it's a risk I take because I believe my interest in him will serve me well with potential employers, and bringing my own destroyed copy would be out of the question. While in the waiting room I read from where I left off and, once again, have an unbelievable urge to hurl the book across the room. I restrain myself, but possibly the men sitting on either side of me can feel my anger, feel my body tense. From that point on I only pretend to read, instead using the time to eavesdrop.

The room is full, it seems they're interviewing a lot. Many of them know each other, have worked together in the past, and their conversations are friendly yet empty. If I get the job I will also need to talk this way so I listen carefully: sports, porn, a few of them have travelled and they speak about deserts, sand and heat, about burqas and exotic prostitutes. There are many terms, mostly slang, that I don't understand. From the context I believe these terms refer either to guns or vehicles, except for the filthy ones that I generally know already. I make mental notes, planning to look things up later, still pretending to read. Once inside, the interview is straightforward. I make a good impression, but I'm not as experienced as many of the other candidates. From the way they explain this to me, I have a slight feeling it might even work to my advantage. Perhaps there are placements where they prefer to train people from scratch. I have a dishwashing gig that night and go directly from the interview to the kitchen, where they make fun of me for being all dressed up. I tell them I just came from a wedding, make up a story about the bride mistakenly saying "do I?" instead of "I do." Everyone laughs. I don't know where this story came from, I pulled it straight from thin air. I'm pleased it got a laugh, eased any suspicions arising from the way I was dressed. The story came from my need to defend myself, protect myself. I wonder how many stories in the world emerge in precisely this way.

1.

All of this is not to suggest, even for a moment, that I did not love and respect my father. While some friends might have advised me to edit out the previous hospital scene, it is my intention here to portray my life in all of its nuance and complexity. It is also true that we, all of us, are never quite as complex or clever as we think (or want to be). In this respect I am not so different from anyone else.

The daily operations of a multinational corporation, one of the largest in the world, are understandably complex. How one deals with such astonishing daily complexity is the true test of one's character. If I compare myself to a few individuals in charge of rival corporations, I can see that my approach and style are almost completely contrary to the ruling wisdoms of the day. For example, while most companies aim for constant, year-over-year growth, I prefer periods of relative calm (that sometimes last several years) followed by spectacular bursts of energy and expansion. It is within these sudden bursts, unexpectedly, that the entire world opens up. For a brief window, the impossible feels possible again. It is important that within these bursts, as I like to call them, everything is entirely unexpected, both for me and for my many employees, that our daily reality is suffused with the purer elements of surprise.

Years of careful planning drain an endeavour of energy, whereas the sudden conquests I envision, in actual fact, cannot be planned. That is what we have learned. These endeavours rely on the irrational, on irrational decisions made by so many of the key players involved, myself included. Investors surging forth on violent waves of excitement or falling away when blindsided by off-kilter fear. Rival CEOs or executives having no idea how to react to an energy, a way of thinking, they have no previous interior experience of, panicking, signing up or caving in. When it all happens fast, the entire landscape can be rearranged before anyone realizes what has happened, in best-case scenarios to my considerable advantage. Of course, all of these strategies, these desires, can easily backfire. Nonetheless, these are the risks, the challenges, the gambles, upon which my heart thrives.

A few weeks ago I was on the street and saw two children fighting. I like to watch children fight. One learns so much about human nature in the different ways each child enters the fray. Do they wait for an opening or charge forward without thought, take the punch like gasoline poured on the fire of their blind rage or dodge every blow as if not getting hit was the sole accomplishment possible. These children were younger than most, and they were laughing. They found their own pre-adolescent brutality almost ludic, so I assumed they must be friends. However, their friendship didn't prevent them from doing damage. One of them was bleeding from the face—so much blood I couldn't spot the wound—and he was laughing, head-butting, working to get as much of the blood on his opponent as possible. Until the other one, the one not yet bleeding, grabbed the blood-soaked jacket, managing to rip it straight up the seam, and they both stopped cold, stopped laughing, froze in tableau. "You ripped my jacket," the bloody one said, as if not sure what his reaction should be, as if his opponent had broken some unspoken rule. It was a serious moment, unexpected. You never know what will happen, what might cause the dynamic to shift.

2.

Didn't get the job but still have two more chances. I've been fully immersed in my private security research and am confident I will do even better next time, at the next interview, that each one will be better than the last. At the same time I'm considering other strategies. If I can't work as his bodyguard, there must be other ways to get close, as a servant in his home or waiter at some function he is scheduled to attend. Luck—the good luck that is involved in getting any sort of gainful employment within the current dreadful state of our economy—will be one thing, and I do hope that I have some. However, careful planning, searching for every possible opening or opportunity to get close to him, to get the piano wire close enough to his throat, will be much more important.

When I was a child, we had a piano in the house and I would play every morning for three hours. If something happened, for example if I overslept, and one morning could only play for two hours, I would spend the entire day feeling things had gone wrong, practice an extra ten minutes for the next six days in order to make up the loss. I don't know if I had the natural talent to become a concert pianist. I had dedication and never faltered. Today, I could easily give piano lessons and make more money than I do washing dishes, have an easier life, but then again I can't because the memories are too painful. When the ones I loved needed me most, when it was time to fight, I was off somewhere playing piano for money, completely detached from their needs. That's so long ago I barely remember, have blocked it out. Now I'm focused on other questions, more pressing concerns, related yet brought into the present, since that tragic story was just one among thousands; similar things happen every year, and it's getting worse.

I am trying to remember the last time I played piano, guessing it was about fifteen years ago. In fact there was no last time, no clear decision to stop. Only new obsessions that gradually devoured my days so there was eventually no time for anything else. Still, I would like to recall the last clear memory I have of sitting in front of a piano to play. There was a competition; it might have been my last, but possibly there were a few more after. I believe I may have won, or at least come very close. I feel I had made an unusual choice as to what I played, Rachmaninoff or Scriabin. One never wins with unconventional choices, but I was long past the point of caring. As I played my thoughts weren't on the score, weren't on the notes, weren't on the beautiful instrument in front of me. All I felt was anger, an anger larger than music, larger than the world. My fingers hit the keys with an intent to smash them, to tear the piano to shreds. I didn't hear the applause, sat at the piano and stared straight ahead. Someone had to come take me off stage, walk me away from the piano like they were helping an elderly relative up the stairs. That perhaps wasn't the actual last time I played, but it might as well have been. My success meant nothing when placed alongside the realities of the day.

Today, while washing dishes, some music came over the radio. There wasn't a radio in the kitchen, so I'm not sure exactly where it came from—from a car parked on the street just outside the door or another restaurant kitchen across the alley— but I knew that music, had played it many times. Strangely, I could not remember which composer, nor the composition, and felt the melody press against me like a skin I had long ago shed. There was a time when I could have told everything about this music, and now all I knew was that it was something from my past. I listened, always knowing what note would come next, and felt pride at how much I had now forgotten. I had severed myself from the finer things, from sentimental resonances and connections that might later hold me back, might prevent me from doing what needed to be done. And yet I still enjoyed hearing this music, in a rather workmanlike performance by a pianist who I believe had never suffered a day in his life. It was a ghost from the past and I didn't mind. It said to me that the world still exists.

I must have stopped to listen because moments later my boss was yelling at me, telling me to get back to work, these dishes won't wash themselves, etc. I try to keep my behaviour in the kitchen as normal and average as possible, so I chided myself for this moment of drifting away. For the next four hours I washed dishes with absolute calm efficiency. These jobs are only to survive and stay out of sight, a hiding place until the time comes to act. Sometimes I pretend that I don't miss my former life, but this is also a mistake. Of course I miss it. I would be stupid not to. It was so much gentler, so much more pleasant, than the life I live today. It is only a matter of focusing on what is most important, on the urgent matters at hand. Each man has to decide: a pleasant, empty life, or a difficult one but with meaning.

When I got home I was exhausted, as is always the case after a dishwashing shift. I lay in bed but couldn't sleep, so instead fantasized about the future, what it would be like if we managed to strike down ten billionaires, in seemingly unconnected killings, spread out over the course of several years. How, once the pattern became clear, journalists would speculate, what they might say about such an unprecedented phenomenon. Some would condemn it; perhaps the press would feel forced to condemn it unanimously, but so many others, people from all walks of life, would feel an excitement difficult to describe, a sudden newfound sense of possibility, the energy of modern violence focused on a cause, towards justice. A warning shot fired against those who wish to debase our world. Of course, all of this is only fantasy. Who knows what will actually happen once the piano wire has done its work. But I need these fantasies to stay focused, to maintain hope that my plan, however difficult to achieve, is for the best, that some new energy will be released through my actions. I need to imagine what is possible.

1.

Allow me to describe a board meeting, not a typical one, but a telling instance nonetheless. Quite early in the meeting, a chief marketing consultant, someone new who I did not yet know very well, launched into his clearly prepared lines, that sales in some areas were down by between two and four per cent, but he also had the solution. He spoke for a while, about packaging-marketing synergy, new techniques for making products leap off the shelf, before I interrupted. He wasn't doing badly, managing to more or less hold the interest of all present, but I had no patience for him; the scale of his reflections was too narrow. "There are two ways of playing this," I carefully explained to the room. "We can try to regain some traction in already played-out, oversaturated areas, or we can search out new energies, blast forward into markets that, at the moment, perhaps do not even exist. If we think of profits as a map, where on the map is no one else going? This is where the real gold is to be found. None of this two or three per cent bullshit."

The room always falls so silent after one of these jags of mine. Everyone feels they should deliver but no one knows what or how. For me, that's always been the sweet spot, this not knowing, at the foot of a mountain, the only thing ahead an incredibly steep climb. You can barely see the mountain from where you're standing and have little idea how long or arduous the journey might be. But you know the journey will test you, that something will happen, something good or bad, anything. However, a mountain is the wrong metaphor, because we all know what a mountain is. In these moments we are searching for something we don't yet know, and as we move towards it, we are always unsure whether or not it will actually generate profit. It is a gamble and the more you gamble the more you win.

Slowly the board meeting changes course and brainstorming begins. In the markets where we are currently losing traction we have so many products and services available, a million possible starting points any one of which could suddenly spark some new direction. Traditionally, a board meeting is not the proper place for this speculation (we have specialists in all of these areas) but I like the board to feel involved, to feel that their ideas matter even when they don't. A board that feels involved is a board that will rarely turn on you, and I prefer all my operations to be mutiny proof.

There is one other moment from this particular meeting I would like to draw attention too. Agriculture remains one of the four pillars of our business model, and one that is unlikely to falter since people will always need food. We have patented just slightly over twelve thousand different seed and crop variations over the past twenty-five years and therefore have a substantial stake within the global playing field. Many of our developmental products in this area remain obscure, things that no one wants, yet we believe, sometimes with little or no evidence, that we may be able to generate a certain degree of demand for them in the future. One such file is 122TOC (let's see if the reader can guess what agricultural product lies behind this abbreviated patent number, and if you look it up on the internet you're cheating). 122TOC had become something of a running joke among the board, the result of a lengthy, research-intensive development process the end result of which seemingly has no practical application whatsoever. It is a tough, difficult to grow, inedible, awkwardly shaped plant of purplish hue. (Some might say much like my prose in this book.) At first we thought it might be used to make rope or cloth, but the price point ratios were exorbitant.

Often, at a meeting, when something doesn't look good, someone might ask whether we're embarking on another road to 122TOC. But at this particular board meeting the joke took another, perhaps more useful, twist. It was suggested we could set up a dummy corporation, an organization that for all intents and purposes appears to be one of our most serious upstart competitors. This 'rival' corporation would work to sell 122TOC seeds to farmers who had consistently rejected our products over the years, perhaps branding them as normal strains of organic wheat or rice. When the crops proved monstrous we would sweep in with the solution, offering, free of charge, to remove all strains of 122TOC from their fields, and in the process replacing them with our own genetically modified examples of rice and wheat. Probably nothing will come of the idea. In a way it is too silly and risky to be worth the considerable effort. But it is an interesting proposition, since it does offer a solution for opening up one of the toughest markets to crack: those who have explicitly refused to make use of our agricultural services, whether for political reasons or simply out of an innate stubbornness (since farmers are nothing if not stubborn, an almost necessary trait in their vocation).

Some might claim such practices are not ethical, and they would have many trenchant arguments in their favour. However, as every child knows, there is a certain charge of pure pleasure in doing something transgressive, in breaking the rules, colouring outside the lines. I won't deny or underestimate the degree to which this frisson is one of the few things that occasionally makes our board meetings enjoyable. There is no harm in speculating, and I believe it is our very willingness to take such thought experiments as far as possible that helps us remain competitive. In a dirty fight one must occasionally punch below the belt, though in this particular instance it seems 122TOC had us on the mat, was a complete write-off. Nonetheless, it was our continual hunger to keep searching for some novel use for this completely useless crop that kept me hopeful, let me know that as an organization we were still hungry and curious, because business is only truly exciting when you manage the impossible. Whatever the costs of the gamble, they are kept in balance by the intensive pleasures of a job well done.

2.

Today I have another interview, the second. I spend the morning reviewing my notes, going over the details of everything I know about security and protection. The basic parameters are not so complex. The main rule is always to think of everything, every possibility and danger, anything that might or could go wrong. One group of agents circle the client at closer proximity, maintaining visual or radio contact, all the while intuitively judging what might be a reasonable distance, not too close but close enough to react at a moments notice, while another group cover the larger perimeter. You carefully check all hallways and passages, every imaginable hiding place. One sweep before the client arrives and another upon arrival. There is also a vast array of technological gadgets, all serving, more or less, one of two general functions: to comb the area for possible dangers or to disarm and/or kill possible assailants. I carefully memorize product names and model numbers, using the same mnemonic devices I once used to memorize musical scores to now assign each product its main and secondary functions.

Then there's the considerable literature on how to avoid future litigation. Some of these documents recommend caution, while others—from what I can tell, the majority available—promote a more reckless approach. If working for an extremely wealthy client, most documents assume it will be reasonably easy to either pay off or threaten the assailant's friends or family members and therefore make any potential litigation disappear. There are many scenarios concerning how to do so. What is important is to protect the core client at all costs. That is what he is paying for.

I take it all with a grain of salt, memorizing for content, thinking how to put all of these terms in my own mouth, make them sound natural and convincing. I know with job interviews it is the energy you bring to the endeavour that counts most. One must appear relaxed, confident and ready to take on any job. The interviewers are the boss, so it's important to strike the right balance between confidence and subservience, to create the image of a man who has the confidence to do what he's told and to do it effectively. I have always had a talent for such situations. I'm hungry for it, want the job, want to win, and my energy falls in line with my desire. There are several hours before the interview and I decide to go for a walk, lose myself in the city, let my mind wander. If I keep studying right up until the moment of the interview, I will arrive too tense. It's better to forget for a few hours, let my mind wander.

I find a park, one I didn't know before, though it's not so far from my apartment, and am amazed how far from the chaos of the city the winding path seems to take me. It's a bright sunny day, calm in the park, and I think: this is perfect, just what I needed. Sometimes, during quiet moments such as this one, I wonder if I could abandon my quixotic undertaking, give it up, and return to living a somewhat normal, though still haunted, existence. I haven't yet gone so far, in practical terms it would still be possible to turn back. I wonder what else I might do with my life if I were to loosen my grip on this over-determined, single-minded pursuit. But I am not able to wonder about such things for long, since I know, for me, there is no turning back. I have made up my mind and am too stubborn to let anything short of death prevent me from reaching my goal.

The park is beautiful—large, leafy trees and flowers in full bloom. I read once that Friedrich Hayek, the forefather of our reigning free market ideology, thought public parks were too socialist, that to enter, one should first be charged a fee. But we still have parks. Things get worse but not as quickly as some might like. I don't really have any positive vision of the future, don't know what kind of world I'd like to some day live in or if it's even possible to achieve something better than this. I only know that the billionaires are attacking us, again and again taking measures that serve no other purpose than to increase their own wealth and debase all other aspects of life. And when you are attacked you must fight back, in whatever way you can.

I arrive at the interview with time to spare. Today the waiting room is sparse, just me and one other guy. A crowded room and an empty room have such different energies, and I feel a certain lack as I wait, a creeping inertia, telling myself that this is a good situation, fewer candidates mean less competition, will increase my chances. The other guy goes in first, his appointment was obviously before mine. As soon as he enters I start wondering about him, thinking about the impression he made in the few minutes we sat across from each other. He was tall, maybe ten years older than me, severe looking. Thinking back, I realize that the first moment I saw him, I had a feeling he might be an alcoholic—something about his complexion, a certain hazy tiredness in his eyes. He wasn't giving anything away, looking straight ahead, only glancing at me once, and yet I took so much unhappiness from his presence. While he's being interviewed, I find myself thinking about him more and more, trying not to obsess, and realize that from the moment I entered the room I already viewed him as a rival. Maybe he needs this job, doesn't know how to do anything else, while I have no interest in the position, am competing for reasons he most likely wouldn't understand or care about. A few minutes later he comes out, smiles at me, says something quick and pleasant, that they're nice in there and I have nothing to worry about. Maybe he was just nervous before the interview. Maybe I was reading too much into his nervousness, letting my own nervousness influence my perceptions. These are the kinds of mistakes, small errors in judgment, I will not be able to make in the future.

1.
I feel absolute loyalty for the men and women who work for me, but friendship is clearly something else. If a man has one or two close friends over a lifetime he's doing well, and there is one friend in particular I've always considered my closest. Emmett was like a son to me, though the difference between our respective ages was not so great. In an environment and

position where it is frequently difficult to trust the endless sycophants who flock around, he was often my bedrock, an eternal confidant who had my back when my better judgment was not in my own best interest. I am not a humourless man, but at the same time, no one has ever accused me of being a great comedian, while Emmett is one of the funniest individuals I have ever known, and in that way we each continuously contributed to the balancing out of the others' minor social lacks.

I prefer to do legal business, but of course a fair bit of the illegal stuff also runs through the books, as it does with any large corporation. What has always been important, even crucial, is that if there is black money to be found somewhere within our organization, I know absolutely nothing about it, in order to prevent future liability. Emmett has always been one of the many employees careful to shield me from specific details of our more questionable pursuits, an undertaking he regularly achieves with effortless panache. For example, during several investigations I was able to testify, even attached to a lie detector, that I knew little or nothing regarding the aspects of our business being investigated. For this I genuinely have Emmett to thank.

And while I consider him one of my closest friends, and also the clear favourite among my many lawyers, it is equally important that I treat everyone within the organization as if they were family. Even a few minutes of my time, to ask what file they are working on or how their kids are doing at school, can serve to put a human face on what, at times, might threaten to become an overwhelmingly bureaucratic daily routine. What is a corporation if not a few million individuals who can be charmed and coerced to work even harder? Since I don't have Emmett's substantial humour to fall back on in these small, daily interactions, I generally try to keep things simple, keep the questions coming, make a show of my interest in the details of their life. Since I have literally thousands of these conversations every year, I cannot remember everything, but you would be amazed at how many things I do remember.

Over the years, watching Emmett work a room has also proven instructive. I certainly can't match him joke for joke, but I can watch and learn, and I will admit, on occasion, to stealing a few of his best lines. There have even been those embarrassing moments when, standing beside him at some corporate function, Emmett has witnessed me telling one of his jokes as if it were my own, and knowing who signs his cheques, played along, laughed along with everyone else, though I know the difference between a real Emmett laugh and a fake one and, on such occasions, the laughs were definitely false. But he would never chide me for such small abuses of our friendship, knowing, as he does, that I need the laughs much more than him, that it all comes much less easily to me. I also knew I had an unspoken advantage, because while people laughed at Emmett's jokes naturally, without giving it a second thought, everyone laughed at mine, plagiarized or otherwise, because they felt required too—a fact I try not to think about too often.

Friendship is a strange idea, difficult to quantify and, at times, even more difficult to maintain. Clearly a friend is someone you enjoy spending time with. However, a friend is also someone you continue to support even during periods when they are considerably less pleasurable to be around. The loyalty of friendship often contains a kind of tautology or feedback loop: the longer you are friends the more loyal you become, and the more loyal you become the longer you remain friends. People change over time, and though one cannot help but compare the way one's friends are today with the ways they might have been in the past, friendship requires that such comparisons must never diminish, or tarnish, the basic steel of the relationship. There is that expression: you can choose your friends but you can't choose your family. Yet with friends one has had for a very long time there is a sense in which one cannot choose them either, in that you cannot choose the ways in which they develop, cannot choose the person they have become.

In the elevator a few days ago, an employee rushed in just as the doors were closing. It was only me and him in there; usually the elevator is more crowded, and I recalled meeting him once before, that his name was Jim, he worked in accounting and had two children. (These are the kinds of details I pride myself on retaining.) I asked how his children were and Jim said his daughter had just begun first grade. I made a few quick jokes, before the elevator reached his floor, not particularly funny, about how I wouldn't mind heading back to first grade myself, at my age nap time was starting to look pretty good again, real corny shit. But I felt relaxed saying it, as he laughed, only because he felt he had to, an ingratiating fake laugh that I also didn't mind. In the ways I felt relaxed I knew I was channelling Emmett, who would have told much funnier jokes and told them more naturally. I felt happy in that elevator, for that brief minute, telling corny jokes, confident they didn't have to be any funnier than they were because, at the end of the day, I run this place, with all the advantages I have earned over the years and deserve, and I believe this feeling of happiness had something to do with friendship.

2.

The first couple of questions are gentle. I breeze through them easily, mentioning a few lessons learned on past (made-up) jobs and how, psychologically, I believe I'm built for a life in security, oriented towards details, fastidious, acting swiftly when the moment requires it. They seem pleased with my answers, friendly. I even manage to make them laugh with a story about an operative I used to know who always checked everything three times, so we called him Goldilocks (which drove him crazy). As I'm telling the story it feels like something that really happened to me, not something I read somewhere, and this feeling of honesty gives me confidence. If I believe my own stories perhaps they will as well.

I've once again brought along the book, the autobiography, and they notice it at my feet, sitting atop my briefcase (where I carefully placed it to incite pertinent questions). This is where my problems begin. No, I didn't realize he was one of their main clients. Yes, I have admired him for a long time now. I respect many important, successful men, believe them to be strong leaders for society, important examples for us all. Yes, I like his biography, find it informative and honest (at this point I'm gritting my teeth slightly, hoping it doesn't show). No, I didn't realize their organization was mentioned in the book, it seems I haven't gotten that far yet. And as I'm answering these questions, lying through my teeth as mildly and honestly as possible (knowing the best lies are those closest to the truth), I begin to realize they are also angry about the book at my feet, that their mention within it must not be entirely positive, and even though he is one of their more substantial clients, in their way they also hate his guts, in a different way from me since, for them, it has even more to do with the grind of recent personal experience. They have met him, dealt with him on a daily basis, while I have not.

I change topics, trying to salvage what I can of the interview, asking some practical questions I hope will be as neutral as possible: How many people work for their organization at any given time? What do they think is an ideal number of employees for a small and for a large operation? Is there any additional material I should read concerning their company? It's no use, they have already lost interest in me. It is as if, by bringing the book along with me, I have aligned myself with someone they are disgusted by. Ironic, since he is also the man I am most disgusted by, the man I want to kill. But it is too late to admit my distain for him. I should have been more cautious in my previous answers. Now it would seem that I was changing my opinion only to please them.

The moment I step out into the reception area I feel crushed, like I might fall suddenly to the ground, crumple into a small heap. I do my best to regain myself, smile at the young man waiting for the next interview, repeat what the previous applicant said to me as he was leaving, that they're nice in there and he has nothing to worry about, but fear I don't sound particularly convincing. They are nice and he has nothing to worry about, but my cause is already lost.

As soon as I'm out of the building, a few blocks away, I violently rifle through the pages to find the mention. It takes me a while, its just a couple sentences quite close to the end, not nearly as negative as I first suspected, though I can see why they were offended. I have a dishwashing shift in an hour and consider calling in sick. I do feel sick, not sure I'm up for much of anything, but think better of it. I must continue to give an impression of steady normality in all aspects of my life. Irregular behaviour is suspicious. I must get through each day without attracting attention, the perfect picture of normality.

An hour is enough time to walk to the restaurant, and I slowly make my way there, calming myself as I go. As I walk, the irony of what just occurred grows steadily in my mind. Also the strange logic of it, of my own naïveté. It makes sense that the man I want to kill has also pissed off some of his colleagues, some of the people he has worked with over the years. If he angered me back when I had barely heard of him, it makes perfect sense that he has angered others as well. In this sense, bringing the book to the interview was the most stupid thing I could have done. It's as if I was so sure I was unique, special, the only one who hated him, and when you are certain, you are always wrong. I should have assumed that whatever I felt, many others felt as well, not taken unnecessary risks.

Suddenly a detail from the interview, one I barely noticed at the time, comes into focus. The first moment they spotted the book at my feet, one of the interviewers, the woman, her first impulse was sarcasm. I'm trying to remember her words more exactly, something like: 'I see you're reading our majesty's treatise,' absolute sarcasm, disdain in her voice. And then I went on to say I liked it and admired him, as I had planned to say before I arrived. There was a moment when I could have saved myself, picked up on their attitude and followed it, matched my tone to theirs, but I was too slow, was somewhere else, not alongside the situation but falling back on my incorrect, preconceived ideas. I must learn from this, every mistake is a lesson. I must not follow some previously memorized score, but read each new moment for what it is, pick up on the signals that will allow me to open things up to my best advantage.

There is not just one road towards my eventual goal; there are hypothetically many, but I must not let any more opportunities slip away.

By the time I reach the restaurant I am once again calm, on time for my shift, and the endless, repetitive washing of dishes calms me further. Others in the kitchen might feel I don't wash the dishes quickly enough, but I am steady, unwavering. Everyone can see that the work gets done.

1.

My mother also didn't care much for being poor, and one of the great pleasures of my ongoing success, in the years before she died, was to considerably improve her financial situation, give her a taste of the life she always dreamt of but that previously remained beyond her grasp. I remember, as a child, listening to her complain. It is only recently I've realized the degree to which her small daily comments might have influenced my worldview. Sometimes, as an exercise to make the boredom pass more quickly, I would place her complaints into four basic categories: 1) Her friends from school now had more than us. 2) We had enough to eat, but never enough to eat well. 3) Life was for enjoying, but how could we enjoy with so little. 4) She works and works, but nothing ever improves. She had hundreds of new ways to make these basic points, plus occasionally a few others, often in a manner that had us doubled over with laughter, and I would marvel at the variation, wondering which of my rather simplistic categories best suited each new complaint. My father would more or less ignore this daily roll call of life's shortcomings, saying we had each other and what more did we need, stepping aside (since so much of her disappointment was directed towards him), but I took every word to heart.

My mother lived fifteen years longer than my father. I have always believed women were better than men: tougher, wiser, more strategic. Statistically, when a man's wife dies, the man drops only a few years later, while women are far more likely to outlive their men by a substantial margin. This is only one sign, out of hundreds, of women's greater inner strength. After her husband died, my mother genuinely came into her own. It was a beautiful thing to witness, how she finally came out into the world. This coincided with a moment at which money stopped being a problem for us, and she could spend it with the best of them. Strangely, on average, I don't spend so much. I like good meals, the convenience of limousines and planes, but have relatively few expensive possessions. Of course, a frugal month for me might be a lifetime's wage for a member of some particularly impoverished nation. But such imbalances are a natural, one might even say glorious, part of modern living. When I think of money and how so much has come my way, how aspects that were once impossible have since become habit, and the relief with which my mother encountered this newfound ease, my next thought is always about how hard I have worked. Because, I believe, I work harder than anyone I have ever met. Of course, most of us, the assholes, believe such things. It is the mantra for my class. But, in my particular case, it is also true.

My mother didn't have to work for the windfall she received, but she did raise me, which I assure you was plenty work enough. We were never close, especially as I got older, but from the moment I could bridge the chasm between us with money, everything became easier. A conversation with my mother generally involved her speaking a great deal and me remembering to turn off my phone for a few hours while she went on. But with family you have no choice, you are bound to them for life. Perhaps it was because I found the conversations so tedious that I never got tired of buying her things, of the pleasure each new item so obviously generated. If it is true that purchases have never been such a great pleasure for me, that I prefer to earn, the least I could do was to enjoy the activity vicariously through her.

The other reason we weren't closer is that I was always too busy working. Now that she is gone, I of course regret this. Even if it was often endlessly boring, it still would have been better to have had more time. But work was, and remains, the absolute priority. An average day for me begins at five a.m. with one-on-one reports from a few top executives regarding developments within their division. I try to keep these meetings light and friendly, to create a sense of warmth, a feeling that if they have problems in the future they can always come to me. The early morning start reflects the fact that, personally, I am at my best when I first wake up, an hour at which many of our employees are still groggy. I also believe this gives me an edge.

There is an espresso machine in my office, and for these early morning one-on-ones I generally prepare the coffee myself, instead of having a secretary do so, which is most often the case later in the day. I feel this act of making and serving coffee for an employee, as a psychological gesture, is essential and even fascinating. It's a kind of display: that I am doing something helpful, that I am there for them. There is no milk, cream or sugar to be found anywhere in my office. When you drink coffee with me you must take it black, and I make each portion strong and thick. This also gives me an advantage, since I am accustomed to the harsh caffeine shock, the bitterness, while many of our executives are not.

At times I also schedule these meetings to overlap, paying careful attention to the moment when the next appointment arrives and realizes that the previous one is still underway. Endlessly intriguing how both employees deal with the situation and with each other. After briefly apologizing for the overlap, I'm already at the espresso machine, pulling another shot, observing how it all plays out from the corner of my eye. Often the previous appointment offers to leave and the game is up, but just as often they attempt to negotiate the space of the meeting, taking turns with their presentations or even awkwardly weaving them together. During these moments so much pure competition is present in the room, an absolute charge, sublimated into pretend co-operation or sparking up briefly as conflict. In general, my philosophy is that there can be no business without co-operation, but people must never get too comfortable. Co-operation must never rule the day.

2.

Since I set myself upon my clear and vicious goal, I have been living as frugally as possible. There is a simple rule for making one's economic life viable. It's never a question of how much you earn, only of how much you spend. I eat two meals a day and both are small. A ten-pound bag of rice will easily last me six months. For protein, a few slivers of meat or fish, lentils, steamed dark green vegetables. I eat nothing outside of the house, nothing I don't prepare myself. And, strangely, I never get bored with this relatively monotone diet, instead finding it steady and comforting. The less food you eat the less food you need, the less hungry you are, perhaps displacing the hunger towards other matters. I want nothing around me that might get in the way, nothing that could distract. This simpler life has benefits I hadn't predicted. I feel calmer, more focused, more precise. A billionaire is just a man like any other. I am also just a man. One man kills another in the name of justice. It's symbolic of the fact that all of us, in matters of life and death, are equal. No one is superior and no one is above the law.

The third interview was by far the worst. I'm still turning it over in my mind, trying to recover. They had phoned every single reference on my resumé and easily ferreted out the lies. Nonetheless, I believe I handled the situation well, explaining that I had fallen on hard times, desperately needed the work, and was therefore resorting to tactics that in other circumstances I very much deplore. They seemed sympathetic, but it was difficult to tell how sympathetic they actually were. I remained relaxed, commending them for their thorough detective work, explaining that other organizations had been considerably more negligent, adding that if I were ever to hire a security firm, which seemed unlikely considering my current poverty, they would be my first choice. I found their reply sobering, as they informed me that other companies most likely did the exact same diligent research, but simply didn't see any point in confronting me with their findings. After all, I didn't get any of the other jobs either. I kindly thanked them for their honesty and felt devastated.

Leaving that interview was the first time I seriously questioned my ability to fulfill my stated goal. It seemed I was in over my head before having made even the first step towards it. And then I began to wonder: if they had discovered my lies, if they had found my resumé so full of holes, why had they even bothered to interview me in the first place, then wondered the same thing about the first two companies, if in fact they had also followed up on my fallacious references. I came up with a strange, unverifiable theory. Maybe these organizations require, from time to time, someone who is completely expendable. And hiring someone unqualified, someone who lied on their resumé, might fulfill this necessity, so later they can say it was the liar's fault, he fooled us with his lies, and pack the scapegoat off to jail while the rest of the company remains unscathed. Maybe it was only this scapegoat position I was being interviewed for.

But becoming paranoid gets you nowhere. And now, even though I suspected there was some clear next step I could take, that all was not lost, I was at a complete loss for what kind of next step it might be. I called in sick for my dishwashing shift, and lay down on my small bed, almost unable to move or think. The more untenable one's position, the more tenaciously one clings to it. Absentmindedly, I picked up the book nearest to the bed—his book, the first one I stole, the mangled copy—and flipped through it at random, eventually landing on a chapter about shareholder meetings. I remembered this chapter, since it was the one in which he gloated most pompously, each sentence inserting new, red-hot embers into the fire of my anger. How proud he was of smoothly deflecting shareholder concerns about the financial health of the company, which I suspected was experiencing difficulty only because he was putting the money in his pocket. All the facts and figures he could so easily memorize, recite back to the crowd and distort. How he could use his mastery of these facts and figures almost like a force field, or like a talisman to mesmerize the crowd.

I knew he was a fake, an imposter, since I also knew a little something about showmanship from my days in front of an audience. The way one walks out to the piano, with confidence or hesitation, clearly influences the judges' assessment of your performance. One learns this and, if you want to win, adjusts one's gait accordingly, until your natural walk is no longer your own. If, when you speak, you think not of what you are saying but of what effect it will have on those in front of you, on the crowd, then your words are also no longer your own. You don't know who you are since everything you say or do is designed to have a specific impact. Sometimes, by hesitating slightly as you walk on, you can lower expectations, therefore creating a moment of surprise by opening the recital with a confident first few notes. But this is a dangerous game, since a negative first impression is difficult to overcome.

1.

Often, as the weeks roll on, I get bored. I have always been a restless soul, searching for the next new adventure, the next frontier, and when business settles into business-as-usual, I feel a kind of itch. Then the question is always the same: how can I use it, avoid making the impulsive decisions that have occasionally marred my progress in the past. Every impulse is like an animal, an animal inside that you cannot fully control. How one manages with this inner zoo is the true test of character. And yet it was during one of these itches, these periods of great tedium, that I stumbled upon the first seeds of a particularly inspiring breakthrough.

All of this occurred against another backdrop, an unrelated crisis, preparing for one of the most challenging shareholder meetings in our storied history. A number of misunderstandings had already reached the press, matters that have since been clarified. Yet at that moment it seemed we were being accused of everything from embezzlement to grand larceny. I always spend weeks preparing for each shareholder gathering—I take great pride in the detail with which I am able to respond to any question asked, no matter how difficult—but this time I was really on a tear, researching, memorizing and researching again. I had never prepared for anything so savagely. How, one might ask, could I become bored in the midst of such precarious chaos? It seems I am being slightly loose with the chronology, since it is likely the boredom arrived shortly after the shareholders meeting had already come and gone. And if I consider it further, boredom might not be the right world: more like the hangover after a party. Yet it so resembled my habitual periods of boredom as to be virtually indistinguishable.

The 'hangover after the party' is also a kind of Freudian slip, since it was at an actual party, in fact one of Emmett's many birthday blowouts, that my mind began to wander. While the pretext for the party was the anniversary of my close friend's birth, at the same time we were celebrating our recent victory in court. (I believe I also had some desire to celebrate my own performance at the above-mentioned shareholder's gathering.) But I was bored, bored with continuously being held accountable, continuously forced up against the constraints of pedestrian reality. How could we arrive at a situation where the ball was always in our court?

I was drinking heavily, trying to drink my boredom away, drunkenly riffing on a few of the above-mentioned topics. A guy from accounting joked that we could form a department of employees happy to take the fall, people hired specifically to take the blame if sticky situations were to arise in the future. Such a department would have to be spread out evenly across all other departments in order to be credible, more like a secret society within the organization, the existence of which would only be known to a few, possibly only to me. Now here was a task, the setting up of such a shadow department, that could fully occupy my itch, since such an operation would need to be executed with absolute guile and craft. And while it is true this idea never came into being—I believe the cold reason of sobriety scuttled it, possibly as soon as the next morning—it was nonetheless the beginning of a long period of speculations that, several years later, did lead to concrete results. (There have been occasions in the past when employees were mortified that I'd taken their black jokes seriously enough to make into reality, but this was not one of them.)

There is one other anecdote I recall from that particular birthday (there were so many parties around that time, all the excesses of those years) and I'm not sure how it happened that the judge who had presided over our recent victory-against-the-odds was in attendance. "This wouldn't look good if certain individuals were to see us right now," he said to me in passing. I wasn't sure what he was referring to; I was refilling his champagne glass so perhaps it was only that, but I remember replying that "actually, I think it would look fantastic." Later that night, during a quiet moment when the party was dying down, he pulled me aside and chided me, told me I shouldn't be so glib, we had gotten off this time, by the skin of our teeth, but next time we might not be so lucky, the usual sort of thing, a friend telling a friend what was or was not in his future best interest. But I was having none of it. "What good is life if you can't make a few carefree jokes?" I remember patiently explaining, possibly raising my voice as I did so. The world was full of dangers, full of journalists who wouldn't mind making a quick buck at anyone's expense, but when it was time to laugh, time to enjoy, we shouldn't let anyone stop us. What was the use of victory if you couldn't turn it into pure pleasure when the need arose to let off a bit of steam? I could tell he didn't agree, but I was drunk and he humoured me the best he could. And what's more I didn't mean a word of it. I was bored. Glib jokes, my own or from others, were boring. Making drunk judges unnecessarily nervous was boring. And I had no idea what adventures still lay in store.

2.

I had bought precisely one share, and was therefore a shareholder, well within my right to attend the annual meeting. I was nervous they would turn me away at the door, that my limited credentials would prevent me from making it in, but soon realized whoever was at the door couldn't have cared less as he passively waved me through. I sat in the large auditorium with hundreds of others. It would be the first time I would see him in person. I wondered how I might react, if my body would tense as he walked on stage, if I would cry out in anger at some particularly obnoxious statement.

But first a series of boring speeches, starting with one that outlined each of the divisions and their relative financial health. Much like I had felt back when I was filling my small apartment with annual reports, now, as I listened, every figure, every profit, every explanatory clause, hit my ears soaked in blood. I wondered whose lives had been ruined in these profits—through long years of barely paid labour, through environmental illness, through families torn apart, through stolen resources that could have easily been put to better use.

Many divisions had to be accounted for and, as I suppose they claimed every year, all of them had achieved record profits, all the usual bullshit. Yet the room warmly received each statement, whitewashed history of the recent past, experiencing every figure as another dollar in their disembodied pockets, politely applauding. If I listened closely it was only vague numbers and vaguer facts, completely detached from how such business transactions took place in the actual world, how they struck people's lives, how they cut into the earth. If I understood correctly, the divisions were entertainment, food and biotechnology, natural resources, banking and investment, communications and what seemed to be some sort of private military, though no one directly said so. The various euphemisms for killing were not particularly ingenious. He ran through it all so quickly, like he was running through the world with his words and slides, like the world was running out.

Next was another man in a bland suit for the projections, possible futures for each division and the organization as a whole. Fuck, he must have thought he was smooth up there, with his endlessly colourful array of charts and statistics, again and again hard-selling how every aspect of business was going to improve, and if no improvement was forecast then quickly proposing adjustments that would make it all better, then predicting further improvements based on these adjustments. And yet as I listened I couldn't hear even a smudge of reality in his approach, in his economic ontology, in his pure spun computer models of pure fantasy, where only money mattered and everything else was either a resource or an obstacle. All he talked about was the future and there was no future. There would be no future if people like this, language like this, was in charge.

A sentence caught my ear and I wrote it down in the small notebook I'd brought along, not his exact words but something like: "On our current trajectory we project a three-fold increase in primary markets, with slight discrepancies for profit margins during periods of political instability." And I thought, on our current trajectory I predict war, famine, general human misery and eventual extinction. Or I thought, yes, political instability, by which he might mean war, famine, general human misery and eventual extinction. But people have been predicting apocalypse from the beginning of time. It's a prediction that leads nowhere. Some kind of wishful thinking. Some day a real rain will come and wash all the scum from these streets. I cannot be that rain. I can only kill one man. One miserable death that I dream will have many positive resonances far into the future. There is no use worrying about extinction. I return my attention to the presentations at the front of the room.

But I have already missed something. They are announcing the man in charge, the man I came here to see. He is already walking on stage, and I feel nothing; no anger, no sadness, no violence. He is just a man, almost a joke or self-parody. The way he speaks is likable and friendly, but of course I do not like him. He knows how to work the crowd. They have laughed at three of his jokes and he's barely started. I know he did not write those jokes himself. He even admits in his book that he's not naturally funny. He explains that he'll keep his remarks brief so there will be plenty of time for questions, and that his colleagues have already done such a good job of telling us everything we need to know. He says he has never been so good with facts, with projections, with technical details. For that he hires the best people in the business and leaves them alone to do their thing. (Though he also mentions that none of his top executives ever forget their ongoing responsibility to the shareholders.) What he has always been best at is vision, expanding, taking risks, risks that result in success and profit. I can imagine him under investigation, claiming he didn't know this or that technical detail and therefore cannot be held accountable. And then the usual bullshit about how no corporation exists without vision, that a business must not be a faceless, soulless entity but instead must be visionary. I'm not counting, but I think he says vision or visionary at least a dozen times.

During the questions I notice a subtle shift in his persona. I can't quite fix it. It's like every answer he gives comes along with a subtext, the message he's trying to convey: this company is not about me but about you. While during his introductory remarks it was all vision and ego, now it is like he has carefully locked his ego in the backroom, all his charm focused on making the individual asking the question feel important. I see his skill and talent, the masterful manipulation, and feel lost and alone. I am the only one in this giant room able to see him for what he is. To a question about global health risks implicit in biotechnology, he answers that without taking genuine risks, without scientific curiosity, there can be no progress. And while they are always careful to take into account the health and safety of the consumer, it is also important never to be so careful that one fails to question the prevailing wisdom, because if no one had ever done so, we might still think the sun revolves around the earth. And then I realize someone in the audience actually asked something, challenged the implicit validity of one of the divisions, and in some ways the spell is broken. There are others willing to challenge him. In some small way I feel a bit less alone.

1.

The scapegoat department, that party joke I hooked onto for a few golden hours, never came to be. But the basic principle was sound: always have an escape, some way out. This principle has informed all my seemingly unsustainable risks over the years and, within the top tiers of my colleagues, has come to be known either as a 'limited hangout' or as 'positive dominoes.'

A limited hangout is a white lie designed to lead seamlessly into another white lie, which in turn logically evolves into another misleading statement, etc. It is where you hang out, but only for a while, just until you can escape into the next useful half-truth. It is a way of controlling the narrative virtually forever. As soon as one hangout starts to thin, there is always another you can conveniently step into or towards. You are therefore never trapped and never painted into a corner. Positive dominoes works in a similar way: as each domino topples it sets off the next.

What is most important about a limited hangout or positive domino is that you always remember it is only a hangout or domino, never start to believe that it is an actual fact or reality. As you can imagine, at times this leads to certain confusions or even difficulties. One might wonder why I am so forthcoming with trade secrets that might be seen to compromise essential facets of our business procedure, and perhaps also make me appear not so sharp from an ethical standpoint. Let me address these concerns in a few different ways. Firstly, I plan to retire soon. I'm proud of my achievements and certainly not ashamed of my shortcomings. Business is business; it is tough and one must possess almost infinite guile in order to prevail. With everything I've done, I am cognizant of the fact that there are others out there doing far worse. More importantly, these revelations (and others you will find in this book) are in and of themselves a kind of limited hangout. They are the things I tell you to distract from other things I may not be revealing. (Or maybe there is nothing else. That is the point: it is impossible to know.) Since what are a few small lies, a few small dominoes, in a global business environment of perpetual scandal and corruption. I firmly believe that, when history compares my habits to the rest, we will come out relatively spotless.

I often judge my top executives by carefully watching how they manoeuvre their way from one domino to the next. In this Emmett was the absolute best. To watch him slip out from an official position and effortlessly slide into the next, even when the contradictions between the two were glaring, with a joke for every step of the way, the room always filled with laughter, was a spectacle of great beauty. One time we were in some nautical mess concerning oil. In the panic of the moment, counting as one of the more severe errors in judgment we have made over the years, we too quickly and clumsily decided that the first domino would be the fact that the captain was drunk. When the captain threatened to sue, and it quickly became obvious it was a lawsuit he could easily win, leaving us wide open to a series of much more expensive litigations, a brief period of public relations chaos ensued, and it was only the quick wits of Emmett, while looking through the list of casualties, that realized all we needed to do was find the highest ranking member of the crew who was both dead and had no immediate relatives. Miraculously this turned out to be the captain's first assistant, and it was fairly easy for us to admit that at first we had made an unfortunate mistake, that it was actually the assistant who had drunkenly steered the tanker into the rocks.

This domino didn't last long, but was enough to buy some time, to get us out of a particularly tight spot. And the ease with which Emmett steered us from one position to the next was breathtaking, joking again and again about our own incompetence, how it was we who had made the drunken mistake, how he would check every drawer for the telltale hidden flask, displacing the difficultly from the spill itself to a clerical error in which we somehow managed to think that the first assistant was the captain himself. For anyone watching carefully, it would have been easy to spot the trick but, in such moments of news-frenzy-chaos, it is often the case that no one is watching closely enough. Or at least no one with enough power to break the story. Because, at the end of the day, for everyone involved, the oil must continue to flow. Emmett stayed strong for the entire crisis, working behind the scenes, spinning one clean-up fiasco into the next new brilliant strategy for how to separate crude from water. Of course, we had every intention of cleaning things up to the absolute best of our ability. We only needed to buy ourselves as much time as possible.

As this example illustrates, a limited hangout or positive domino is never an end in itself, only ever a means, in this case to buy us time to figure out how to thoroughly clean up the spill. But time is a precious commodity, perhaps the most precious, and therefore every domino counts.

2.

Afterwards I found myself standing in the parking lot. I don't know why I was standing in the parking lot. I didn't know what else to do. I was so angry and lost. I wanted to process everything I had seen and heard but couldn't. I watched the cars of the shareholders drive away, one after another, back to their houses and their lives. Logic tells me that he won't walk out into the parking lot, that he has some other way out, a back or side door, but perhaps secretly I am hoping that any moment he will walk by on the way to his car. I have the piano wire in my jacket pocket. I could approach him, shake his hand, congratulate him on another masterful performance. He will be surrounded by bodyguards but maybe there would still be some way for me to get in there. I know this is not a good plan. I will need to come up with something better, more skilful, with careful planning and a touch of strategic genius. But what could that possibly be?

I look up and realize there is another man standing in the parking lot. He is far away from me, right on the other side, as far away from me as possible. And then I have a completely insane thought: if he is standing around in the parking lot, perhaps he is here for the same reasons. Perhaps he also wants to kill that asshole, and then we could work together. When I have insane ideas sometimes I feel I am losing my grip on reality, that my anger has twisted my brain one twist too far, but I suppose there is no harm in having strange thoughts from time to time. And I desperately want to talk to someone. It seems to me like it's been a hundred years since I've had a real conversation. I can barely even remember the last time. I think to myself: already we have one thing in common, we are both eerily stalking the parking lot long after the shareholder meeting has ended. This gives me a way to start. I can ask him why he is standing around. If his answer sounds honest, and if he asks me the same question in return, I realize I might answer honestly as well, how desperately I suddenly want to tell someone of my plan. It's terrible to have a secret.

I start to walk slowly towards him. As I do so another possibility, far more reasonable, occurs to me: that he is a private security guard paid to watch the parking lot, in fact paid to stop people exactly like me. Then what I might be about to do seems even more insane: admit to a security guard that I am planning to kill the man he's being paid to protect. As I get closer it is like a hallucination, in that I actually recognize him. There was a section of glossy photos in the middle of the book, many of the photos including a broadly smiling Emmett, and this, the man at the other end of the parking lot, is Emmett. Ten or twenty years older but definitely him. Now he is not smiling and, from reading the book, or at least reading between the lines, I believe I know why. I think: this is my one chance to meet someone completely sympathetic to my goal, someone who also has a reason to want the billionaire dead. Here was a capitalist who knows, from personal experience, that everyone is expendable.

I think about what my first line should be, how I should introduce myself. I already know so much about him and he knows absolutely nothing about me. But I wonder if the things I know about him are actually true, since, the more I think about it, the more I realize that so much in that book must be lies, cover-ups and exaggerations. Of course in every lie there is a grain of truth. I decide to test the waters slowly, feel him out. He must also be filled with anger but that does not mean the anger is on the surface, does not mean it can easily be reached. And then the strangeness of the situation strikes me anew. What the fuck is he doing standing out here in a parking lot? It makes no sense. Even if he is no longer working, he must have money coming out of his ears. He doesn't need to stand around out here alone.

I reach him and ask for a cigarette. I don't smoke and fortunately he doesn't either. I just wanted to say something normal to get the conversation rolling. I ask if he was in there, at the meeting, and he says that he was. I ask him what he thought and he's non-committal, doesn't say much. I'm hoping he'll ask me what I thought but he doesn't. Maybe it's good he doesn't, because if he had I'm not quite sure what I might have said. Then, at a loss for where else to go, I tell him that I recognize him from the book, from the pictures inside the book. It takes a moment for him to realize which book I'm referring to, but when he does his expression rapidly sours. I'm about to say something critical about the book, to win him over a bit, but stop myself, not sure how critical, or even vicious, to be. Instead I decide to wait, see if he says anything more. He looks around, perhaps waiting for me to go away. I let it sit for a long time, hoping that if I stay there long enough he'll get used to me. After a while I tell him that, though I don't know the details, I'm pretty sure he got a raw deal, and I've certainly gotten a raw deal once or twice in my life so I know how much it sucks. Again a long silence. I think he might say nothing else for as long as I stand there, but nonetheless I wait.

After a while he looks at me and starts to talk. He says that the book was unfair, it was unfair how it portrayed him and, if the settlement hadn't forced him to remain silent, he would write his own book to set the record straight. He now regrets even agreeing to the settlement, but at the time it felt like he had no choice. Still, every time he thinks back to how he had been paid off, it almost kills him. For a few million he must live in disgrace for the rest of his life, unable to speak honestly about the things that have mattered most to him. He tells me he can't believe how bitter he has become, how sour, that all his life he had been one of the most fun, one of the happiest, one of the most joyous people anyone knew, and now he was like a crumpled piece of steel covered in rust. The way he describes himself, a 'crumpled piece of steel covered in rust,' I don't think I'll ever forget those precise words or his voice as he said them. This was a man who, back when he had a job, had done so many corrupt and awful things, ruined so many lives, stockpiled so much cash and turned every dirty trick to get it. There was no reason for me to feel sympathetic towards him. But I was glad I felt sympathy because I needed his help, and it's much easier to ask for help when some sympathy is present.

1.

We had a young intern in one of our departments. Turns out she was an aspiring poet. One day I'm briefly introduced to her and she manages to hand me a sheaf of poems. Wants to know what I think. Now, at the time, I didn't know poetry from a liability report, but I take the poems home and read them to the best of my ability. I like them well enough, and send a short note telling her. A few years later she is already a successful poet, if such a thing can be said to exist. She wins a prestigious award, mentioning me in her acceptance speech, thanking me for the support I gave back when she was a struggling intern. Suddenly I'm getting letters from every poet in the country and they all want money. We have to hire another secretary just to go through the requests. All I did was send a note saying I liked her work—it took me less than a minute to write—but the entire world now thinks I gave her financial support, might soon do the same for them. And that is how our poetry foundation came into being.

As someone who spends the better part of his life figuring out how to make as much money as possible, I believe it is beneficial for us to be closely associated with a pursuit at which it is entirely impossible to make a red cent. It costs us relatively little, since poets don't need much to be happy, and garners small amounts of precisely the right kind of publicity. To anyone who says that we are only in this for the money, we can always reply that, no, we are also in it for the poetry. I no longer have much to do with the foundation. There is a board that every year selects three qualified judges who read through the applications and patiently dole out the awards. But I am sent a pile of books every year, books in which the foundation is thanked for its support, and I do read each of them carefully. Much can be learned from poetry. When it is boring it is boring in an absolute way, and to write poetry that is not boring is a kind of absolute challenge, analogous to the challenge I take upon myself to change things up whenever I begin to find my position dull. Poetry, like business, is full of tricks and clichés. And one quickly learns just how much energy it takes to write a poem that is genuinely surprising.

I also attend the annual awards ceremony and meet each of the poets in person. I believe there is a certain irony in the fact that they are considered colourful, fascinating artists, while we are considered bland, faceless vultures. From a distance, if one doesn't look too closely at our respective attires, it would be difficult to tell who among us is a corporate suit and who a poet. It is rare that a poet says or does anything interesting or outrageous during one of these functions. Usually the function itself is as dull as a board meeting (or at least as dull as a board meeting at which I am not personally in charge). But there was one notable exception.

Along with the regular awards, the foundation gives a lifetime achievement award to an older poet. In the past, this older poet would give a brief speech at the ceremony, though for obvious reasons, reasons you will soon see, we no longer allow this. Because one year the award went to a real radical, and for his speech he thoroughly raked me over the coals. He was good at it too, with precise, clear statistics for every evil thing he claimed we had done, but also jokes, personal jokes at my expense and genuinely accurate jokes about the rapacious nature of our business practices. It was one of the few years I wasn't bored. He even finished by dramatically tearing up our cheque, saying that dirty money and poetry didn't belong in the same room. And this was one of the rare moments you could tell the poets and vultures apart, since most of the poets applauded, while only a few of the suits had the guts. (Perhaps more of our employees would have done so if I had not been present.) His poetry was good too. I still have his books by the side of my bed. Such a clear-eyed view of the disaster in which we live, and yet every page makes room for some humour or joy.

There was some negative press but it could have been worse. A poetry prize is pretty minor as far as news stories go. And in the weeks that followed, when asked, I had my reply well scripted, explained that giving the award to someone so negative was a clear display of our openness, our willingness to be self-critical. We weren't perfect but we clearly weren't close-minded. It wasn't until two weeks later that I had another idea.

I approached the sweetest of the three judges—a bright young woman—and explained to her that despite his performance at the ceremony, which I then admitted how much I had enjoyed, we wanted our fiercest critic to have the money anyway. I asked her, off the record, if she'd be willing to approach him, to find out if he would accept the cash in secret, and that if he did so we promised never to tell anyone. I don't believe there is any shame in the fact that he graciously accepted, as everyone knows the financial lot of poets is certainly not glorious, and he had never managed to sustain a teaching position. Even though we never had occasion to use it, I always felt more comfortable knowing that we had something on him; he had taken a payoff from the mouth of the beast. Much like those of us in business, he too behaved one way in public and a slightly different way behind the privacy of closed doors.

I met him again a few years later and, more out of curiosity than anything else, suggested we get together for a drink. I don't know why he agreed, perhaps also out of curiosity, but we spent several hours together as I paid for round after round of the best scotch in the bar. I was clearly fascinated by him, but had the strange sense he was equally fascinated by me. As far as he was concerned I was the devil itself, but the devil always holds a variety of attractions. As he spoke I could tell he was running through his rhetorical gambits, trying to see if he could convince me of anything, if he could win the day on some small point. He wanted me to concede something, anything, and I tried to explain it as clearly as I could. It wasn't that we disagreed on any fundamental aspects. Of course the profits we made caused harm, both to people and to the earth. Of course the harm was irreparable. From my point of view I didn't see how such facts could be questioned. It was only that I saw nothing wrong with benefiting from things that were harmful. It seemed perfectly natural to me that some would benefit while others would suffer. I saw nothing in human history that suggested anything should, or could, be otherwise.

He thought about this for a long time. I don't know what he was expecting, but nonetheless felt I had caught him by surprise. I wanted to laugh at his expression, since back at the ceremony he'd never been at a loss for words, and now he was so silent. It looked like he was thinking so hard he might burst. Finally he said: "We only think it's bad when it happens to us, or to someone we love."

"We only think what is bad?" I finally asked, since it seemed he wasn't going to offer up much more on his own. I had found a way to shut him up.

"The destruction. The destruction you call business. The natural process of making a profit."

"Is that a poem?" I asked wryly, but he ignored me.

"Have you ever loved anyone," he asked. He was looking straight at me, suddenly sincere beyond belief. I actually didn't know anyone could be so sincere, or could turn that way on a dime. But I was unfazed. I looked at his face. Before I'd thought we were pretty much the same age, but now realized he was at least ten years older than me.

"Yes," I said without missing a beat, "I've loved everyone who's ever worked for me. I love everyone who works for the company."

He didn't reply.

2.

With Emmett, there is always so much silence, the conversations grinding to a halt far more often than they restart. I would think: this is a man who, at some point in the recent past, always had a joke at the ready and yet, in the entire time I've known him, never once tried to make me laugh. Does anyone change so much in such a short period of time? Then again, the book was full of lies and exaggerations. Perhaps his infamous sense of humour was yet another deception.

I was grateful he had agreed to meet with me and that, gradually, some slight, strange friendship was being offered, or even created, between us. His mood was continuously tense, especially when speaking about his old job, the direction in which most of my questions seemed to drift. Other topics were difficult to detect. From what I could see he had few or no interests, so instead there was silence. There were dozens of moments I can clearly recall, points at which I thought to break the silence by revealing my plan, when I was right at the brink of explaining just who I wanted to kill and why. I became more and more certain he would find a way to support me in my endeavour, that he could help. But each time something stopped me.

It is difficult to admit you want to kill someone. To say it out loud. This was the first time I realized that, even though it had been my goal for so long, I had never cleanly admitted it to anyone. Of course, the less people who knew, the less who could stop me. And I believed I should build as much trust between us before confiding. Trust takes time. I had no idea how long was necessary or how I might eventually know. I tried to keep things relaxed. Meetings for coffee. Seeing if there was anything I could say or do that would make him laugh or even smile. (Smiles were rare and I don't think I ever managed a laugh.) Waiting a few weeks before I called him again. I could see he had few friends, that since most of his friends had turned on him he had barely learned how to live without them. When you have money perhaps you don't need friends.

I had known him almost a year before he first invited me to his house. It was the largest, most expensive house I had ever seen, with servants to clean, cook and maintain the grounds, but for the most part it felt deserted, like no one lived there. Room after empty room, the furniture dust-free and silent. It was a warm night, and as we walked up to the balcony, Emmett told me I was the first guest he'd had over in five years. He paused before the number five, counting to himself, calculating just how many years it had been, sounding surprised it had been so long. When he lost his job his wife left him; she had done all the entertaining, he didn't have the knack for it alone. In fact, he wondered if he even had the desire to see people any more. He used to love people, could always make them laugh, but now he wondered if he still had the desire.

That night, after more than a few drinks, he also admitted that when we first met he'd hired a firm to look into me. That he knew about my family, about my years playing piano, about my descent into dishwashing. That he felt partly responsible for what had happened to my family. For the entire time he had known me he'd been trying to find the strength to apologize. He knew an apology didn't mean much—what was done was long ago done, the past couldn't be changed—but he was adrift in his life and, if I were to accept his apology, acknowledge that he had changed, it might be a first step towards some sort of decision.

I wondered what kind of decisions he now wanted to make. I thought this was the moment to tell him my plan but once again something stopped me. I accepted his apology, told him it wasn't his fault, these catastrophes happen all the time. They represent structural problems with society, with the world, that were so much larger than either him or me. I told him it wasn't his fault, since I was still working to further gain his trust, but at the moment he mentioned my family, granting him absolution was not my first instinct. My first instinct was to strangle him then and there. I still had the piano wire in my jacket pocket. My hand instinctively reached for it, just to feel it was still with me. Fortunately he was too wrapped up in his own hesitant apology to notice.

And then I turned the wheel, took us the first few steps towards what might soon be the right direction. Saying that it wasn't his fault because he wasn't in charge. And if we were to blame anyone, logic dictates we should blame the person who ruined his life, who ruined both of our lives. That this was something we very much had in common, him and I, both of our lives had been sabotaged by the same man. And as we began to speak of his former boss, more and more frequently as the months progressed, I could see that in so many ways the man who once screwed him over was still his best friend. Had been his only best friend and in many ways remained so. That even though they hadn't spoken a word to each other in five, ten, I don't know how many years, still somehow the friendship, for one of them at least, had survived. But at the same time this wasn't entirely true.

I began thinking about friendship and betrayal. How one definition of a friend might be someone who was in a position to betray you more savagely, more painfully, than anyone else in the world. I was aware this was not the most common understanding. I'd had friends when I was a child, and later on the competition circuit, but now had none. In some sense Emmett was my only friend, but I knew it wasn't real. My plan was to use him. After I had used him, if everything worked and I was in jail, I did not think he would continue to be my friend. In fact, when I considered the matter, I realized I no longer desired friends. I desired imitators. I wanted to kill a billionaire, and others to imitate by also killing billionaires. Another rough definition: a friend is the opposite of an imitator. A friend will call you out on your bullshit, but an imitator will simply copy it. A soldier is an imitator and we are at war. We need as many soldiers as possible. And we need someone to fire the first shot. Emmett was not a true ally. The way they treated him, he should have become a full-time traitor to his class, but he was not. He was not built that way. Perhaps none of us are. We do what we are told when we are children, and then, to a lesser or greater extent, just keep doing it for the rest of our lives. Perhaps I am exactly the same, since I vaguely remember my father telling me that in the playground, when someone hits you, you have to hit them back. The only way they will ever respect you is if you hit them back, as hard as they hit you, no harder but no less. Autobiography is politics. The only sincere reasons for action are personal.

1.

Where does that expression come from: do unto others as you would have them do unto you. I keep meaning to look it up. Because when it comes time to discuss the one disaster that almost toppled everything, that is the phrase, the explanation, that keeps coming back. Someone, or more precisely a coalition of someones, tried to do unto me as I had been doing unto others since the beginning. My first mistake was not taking them seriously. I did not take them seriously for the worst possible reason, because I had never heard of them. No one had heard of me when I started and I did okay.

They bought up the first blocks so quickly, and with such determination, it should have set off every alarm bell in history. But they were upstarts and instead triggered a rare failure in my imagination, in that I couldn't particularly imagine them pulling it off. We judge ourselves by our unlimited potential, and others by their limited abilities. Before we had even had our first strategy meeting they were up to thirty per cent, and a few days later they owned forty-five. At that early juncture, where they were getting their money from, who might have been backing them, remained a deep mystery, one which I was paying a dozen guys full-time to solve. It was like an alien invasion, completely unexpected and just as inexplicable.

There are hundreds of ways one could disassemble our organization, some of which, from a fairly narrow point of view, might even appear to make it more efficient. If you were to start selling off divisions, the permutations are endless, which ones to sell and which ones to keep. Efficiency has never been a buzzword in the circles that surround me. I prefer risk, experimentation. So their motives were not hard to discern. They wanted to rip my company to bits—fast money for the taking. There were so many different scenarios in which, no matter how ridiculously high the shares rose, the takeover could easily pay for itself. I'm sure their mouths watered as they ran through the projections. What I couldn't understand was how they had managed to remain so secret. A series of shell organizations that we traced, each leading to, as far as we could see at the time, an unrelated owner. The more we learned the less we knew. It was infuriating.

They walked into the meeting, twenty of them, all in black suits. They were like a comedy routine, but by that point I was fighting for my life and didn't find much funny. I had been untouchable for so long, it had been such a long time since anyone had seriously challenged me. It was as if there were a ten-second delay before the fight within me fully kicked in. I realized something at that first meeting, staring at all those cheap black suits and the pudgy faces that topped them off. My sense of reality had slipped. I thought I was out there in the trenches, fighting every day, fighting full-on and giving it everything I had. But what was invisible to me was that so many of the fights were fixed. It wasn't that I couldn't lose. I lost my fair share of battles like anyone else. But it had been at least twenty years since I had been in a fight where I could lose everything. And when there's the possibility you might lose everything, it's a different kind of war. (Of course, in this case, losing everything is only a figure of speech. A whole series of golden parachutes would kick in if they managed to sack me.)

At that first meeting they hinted, more obvious than an out-right offer, that they'd grease my palms if I stepped out of the way. I did my best to laugh in their faces. In retrospect, I can see I wasn't convincing. It was a rare performative failure. They had me backed into a corner and knew it better than I did. There were twenty of them at that first meeting and we were a bargaining team of nine. I made a mental note that at the next session we'd bring at least forty.

For some reason Emmett wasn't at that first meeting, proof that I wasn't taking the challenge seriously enough, but I was sure to have him by my side at every subsequent session. We developed an ongoing routine: every time they came at us with something, I would attack the numbers or fine print, and then Emmett would follow with some small joke attacking one of them personally—something about their appearance, weak breeding or lack of credentials. I knew there must be a maelstrom of insecurities in that room—you don't try to slay Goliath if you're not worried about the size of your dick—and I intended to ferret out these insecurities one by one. You could tell when Emmett hit a nerve: the victim would flinch and then immediately smile, or grimace, or cover in some other way. They had good poker faces for business but not for their personal shortcomings. Because there were so many of them, we could keep moving it around, find the weak links and focus in. After a few sessions, Emmett, who had been monitoring the reactions to his jokes like a hawk, honed in on the three we decided to meet. For legal reasons I will refer to them as A, B and C.

At first, only B agreed, the other two understandably explaining that we should fuck right off, as I too would have done in their position. But at least we had B, the brother of one of the two ringleaders, dragged into the takeover through filial association alone. B had an endless list of hang-ups regarding his brother that we listened to as patiently as possible. Things were moving fast. Offers had already been tendered and a battalion of lawyers were pouring over them with an arsenal of fine-tooth combs. Neither Emmett nor I felt we had ten years to waste serving as B's on-call psychoanalyst, but we kept taking things slow. At least two weeks had passed before he handed us the first useful piece of information. At that time two weeks felt like an apocalypse of waiting.

Our meetings were infrequent, and several times B didn't show up at all. He was terrified of his brother finding out, nervous about being followed. We had a car pick him up, drop him off at the subway where he travelled five stops, then got in a taxi. Sometimes he had travelled half the city before eventually showing up in some hidden-away dive bar three hours late. But we put up with the antics, because we also believed that, if his brother found out, our only source of information would be cut off. After two weeks he mentioned, perhaps not even realizing what a breakthrough it was, that the core of their bid was a one billion dollar family inheritance courtesy of the other ringleader. (The one who wasn't his brother.) Their entire bid reeked of decay, so it made perfect sense that death was at the heart of it.

2.

Then, one day, without my doing anything to set it off, we were having a drink on his balcony and Emmett asked me if I wanted a job. I was about to ask what kind of job when I paused for a moment, realizing I already knew. He was going to offer me a job that would bring me closer to my goal. My goal was entirely unspoken: it is possible he had no idea, but I could feel in the way he asked some desire to help, and perhaps also to remain ignorant of specific details. He said I would need a suit so we went to his closet, found one that sort of fit. He gave me an address downtown, told me to show up at nine ready to work. He already knew I would accept.

I arrived the next day and was ushered to my office, told that because of a favour, about which I should never tell anyone, not even my close friends, they weren't going to interview or train me. I could figure out the job as I went along. The first day I spent filling out paperwork so they could put me into the system. Two weeks later, they handed me my first cheque and a new difficulty arose. I didn't have a bank account. For dishwashing they had always paid me under the table, and I was paying for my one-room apartment in a similar manner. At first I thought I should simply let the cheques pile up on my desk. That is how much disgust and anger I had for their money. I remembered a story I'd once heard about Erik Satie. After he died, his friends went to clean up his apartment, and found every letter they had ever written to him sitting on his desk unopened. I wanted to emulate that story but knew, in the long run, it was a bad plan. I would need a certain amount of cash to pass at the job, so they wouldn't suspect me. To buy a few suits, have them dry-cleaned. I didn't even own hangers. My two pairs of pants and half-dozen shirts were folded neatly on the floor in the corner. I had been placing the one suit that Emmett gave me on the back of my only chair. In the pocket, without telling me, he had placed a wad of cash, I guess to get me through the first couple of weeks. I had been using the money for lunch and nothing else, to make it last as long as possible.

Now that I was working in his former department, my meetings with Emmett had to be kept secret. Emmett was in so many ways *persona non grata* at the organization and no one could be allowed to realize we knew each other. We stopped meeting at his house, and instead met at a series of cheap bars where he felt confident no one would recognize him. I wondered how he knew so many cheap bars; we met at a different one each time. Soon the dynamic of our meetings had shifted, Emmett coaching me on every aspect of the organization, my every question focused on how to get closer to my target. I realized that Emmett had once played the organization like a finely tuned device. He carefully explained how each position functioned, how each employee operated, what they wanted and how to get on their good side. I realized something I found momentarily shocking. Emmett had been excommunicated at least ten years ago, but everyone else, or at least everyone near the top, still had their jobs. You only need one good scapegoat to make a problem go away.

My job consisted of sorting through everything that had been written about the various divisions, summarizing them in a series of cross-filed reports. A pre-propaganda job, since my reports would later be used to strategize what spin might be required for routine publicity, as well as, more importantly, for new initiatives. The only good thing about the job was that my target personally read each of the reports I produced, and if he had any questions he would phone me to ask about them. Since he almost always had questions, I would speak with him on the phone once, twice, sometimes three times a week. It seemed clear to me that if this were to continue, I would soon become a regular presence in his life, and there would be no question that at some future moment he would let down his guard. There remained the slight dilemma that most of our conversations took place over the phone, and I rarely met him in person. But I reasoned it would only take one significant meeting for me to complete my goal, just ten minutes alone with him, and that certainly could be arranged over time. I kept the piano wire with me at all times.

I would record our phone conversations, listen to them at home, analyzing what changes I could make in my approach to further win his trust, listening again and again, some of them strangely more entertaining than others:

—So there's a difference in how the genetics are perceived when one looks at the north versus the south?
—I don't think you'd need my report to tell you that.
—How do you mean?
—Just look at an electoral map. Or get on a bus.
—But how does this relate specifically to food? What's the takeaway?
—Assumed it went without saying. In the south, it's of course: what we don't know won't hurt us. In the north, they want science, hard facts.
—How do you mean: what we don't know? Everyone wants to know things?
—All the southern items lead with an anecdote, usually something local and friendly, and bury facts that might be distressing in the middle of the piece. The reassuring lead colours the rest. Ostrich-style. They're going to accept whatever we give them.

It frequently occurred to me that I was doing some small amount of harm in the world. But I didn't plan to be doing it for long, just long enough to get him alone, and if I was not compiling these reports they could easily hire someone else. I tried to keep the accuracy of my reports well within the bounds of familiar cliché, ignoring any information that might be counter-intuitive and therefore useful. Within the boundaries of my thinking at the time, this served two general ends. If I provided them with only what they already knew, I could comfort myself in the thought that, in my job, the basic values of which I despised, I was doing neither harm nor good, since I was not bringing anything new or unexpected into the system. More importantly, it was unlikely anyone within the organization would ever question my findings, since they all seemed so intuitively obvious and reasonable. I was keeping my head low, would make no waves until the final tsunami that would end it all.

1.

They were a handful of shares away from a majority, had met with the board and charmed them (a board I had always assumed to be safely in my pocket), every piece of evidence pointing to the fact that, in a short number of days, I would be the unemployed laughingstock of the international business press. When you are fighting for your job, your life, for everything, occasionally you might do something you later regret. I am sharing this now, my momentary lapse of judgment, because it's a dirty trick that works, and will always work, no matter how many people know about it or attempt to make use of it, and such things must be out in the open. We already knew an inheritance was involved, an inheritance that could be lost if the deal went sour, and it seemed reasonable that other family members might have also had their eyes on this very large sum, and that we could provide them with lawyers who could assist in their desire to contest the will. We knew nothing about the contents of the will itself or whether any other family members had legitimate claims. We only wanted to cause trouble, slow things down, make their lives as miserable as they were making ours.

Tracking down the family was the most difficult part. At first it seemed all was lost, that our second-in-command adversary had the only legitimate claim, was the only living relative. I'm not sure if it was Emmett or I who first realized that a legitimate claim was unnecessary. Any kind of claim would easily serve our needs. The question was how to make it seem, at least on the surface, plausible. We hired a firm to run computer simulations, looking at dozens of individuals who grew up in the same region as the deceased, with similar backgrounds and family connections. We came up with a list of criteria— age, regional proclivity, net worth, family tree connectivity— and used this list to generate an array of possible 'long lost relatives.' Emmett then spent a week travelling, speaking to each candidate in person, feeling them out to see if they were good actors and how much it would cost to convince them to take a long, hard run at it. This led to three promising contenders, and we assembled a team of top lawyers for each one. Emmett reasoned that the publicity we would generate in the battle over the inheritance might draw some real family members out of the woodwork, and in this we were doing them a genuine service.

As the lawyers were preparing three separate but interrelated strategies to contest the will, it wasn't so much that time was running out, more like all clocks were on fire, since the attack, the plan to rip our company to shreds, was also intensifying. At night I would lie in bed, think we were doing everything right, but why wasn't it going fast enough. They were going to beat us, win the race. I imagined what it would be like to lose everything. What I would do with my life if I was no longer running the organization. Consulting held no allure; to the contrary, it seemed like the purest form of hell. I was a man who needed to be in charge: of his world, his universe, of everything. We required another edge and, once again, it was Emmett who had the brainstorm.

Even though C had refused to meet with us, he still flinched— a painful, severe reaction he was unable to conceal—every time Emmett laid into him during a bargaining session. We believed there must be some way we could make use of him as a weak link. We'd already learned he was their main number cruncher and, in the process of having him followed, also realized he was visiting his doctor several times a week. His medical records were not difficult to obtain, a bad heart exacerbated by the stress of the negotiations. We began to strategize on how to increase his stress to the point he would be forced to drop out. We thought threatening phone calls, at all times of day and night, would be the simplest bet. We then worried they would be too easy to trace back to us, since who else had a motive to threaten an innocent, benign accountant whose only transgression in life was visiting his doctor four or five times a week. However, since millions of heart attacks happen in the world every day, we saw no reason we couldn't find some way to take him to the brink.

There was one particularly tense session that is burned into my memory like my whole life flashing before me. First rumours of new family members seeking their share of the inheritance had just begun to circulate. The enemy second-in-command was visibly agitated, we had caught him by surprise, but he had worse venom to throw in our faces. After some preliminary small talk, he announced that the board had accepted an offer of one hundred and two, and it was time to shift the discussion, to begin talks about who, in the future, was going to manage the company, in what form, on what terms. For the first time in my life I thought I might faint. Even if there was some way to survive, these would be the bastards signing my cheques, calling the shots. I pictured myself following orders, announced I was stepping out of the room, that before we could proceed I needed to speak to each of the board members personally. But at that precise moment I had no intention of phoning anyone. For the past few weeks none of the board members had been returning my calls.

What happened next was without me in the room. I have heard the events described so many times, in so many different ways, that I no longer know what is true and what is pure exaggeration. What I do know is I got in the car and drove, and after twenty minutes of driving took out my phone and called Emmett, who was still embroiled in the session. When Emmett answered I told him we were lost, I'd run out of ideas, all the cards were in their hands, I no longer knew what to do. Emmett addressed me not by my own name but by another, the name of the head of the board. I had no idea what he was up to but tried my best to play along. Yes, the board was planning an emergency meeting for that night. Yes, at midnight. Yes, we were having second thoughts. No, nothing had been signed yet. I was impersonating a man who wouldn't even return my calls, and for the past twenty years everyone had returned my calls as if their lives depended on it. Then I spent ten minutes outlining the various challenges to the inheritance, as Emmett replied: yes, I see. No, we didn't know that. Yes, I suspect that would change several aspects of the deal. I said goodbye. I said we would phone him again after our emergency midnight session. I hung up and continued to drive.

Perhaps they would have immediately phoned the board in an attempt to verify our admittedly rather thin play-acting—they certainly must have been suspicious—but at that moment, in the ensuing chaos and yelling, C keeled over and was rushed to hospital. You need a great deal of luck in business just to survive, and apparently our short test-run of threatening phone calls was more effective than we first assumed, could even be said to have overshot the mark. Even with C on his way to the hospital many on their team wanted to continue. Our side of course couldn't wait to get out of there. At that point, no one from our team had any idea what to make of the phone call. Had our company just been bought out from under us or not?

We worked all night to get the inheritance story onto the front pages of a few small newspapers for the next morning, and made sure each of these papers were hand-delivered to every single member of their team, as well as to each member of our board. For a while we considered printing up a run of fake newsprint, but fortunately this proved unnecessary.

2.

Emmett fed me constant advice on how to win over his former boss. Flattery was possible, but the compliments should be measured and precise, always leavened with just the right touch of humour. Gradually, through trial and error, I learn what makes my new boss laugh, and as I do so he phones more often, looking for distraction, for someone not afraid to take a few gentle shots at him in pursuit of mirth. I can feel him draw closer, but its another six months before I meet him in person.

At that first encounter he takes one look at me, the way he stares making it clear I am not the man he was expecting. I don't know why I'm in his office. I had hoped we would be alone but there are a dozen of us that morning. It is five a.m. and he stands at his beloved espresso machine, making coffee after coffee, bursting with ideas, energy, and those of us with considerably less experience being awake so early, myself included, scatter around feeling lost, like a pick-up game where no one has remembered to bring a ball. When I introduce myself, I can tell he recognizes my voice, that in his head he has already attached the voice to some other face and body, definitely not the one in front of him. Perhaps he was expecting me to look like Emmett. No one else in the room has the faintest idea who I am.

When we all have our coffees he announces that, from time to time, he likes to bring a random group of executives together to brainstorm, whatever drifts through our heads. I look around; we're all thinking the same thing: this is hell, a cross between group therapy and a job interview. But you only have once chance to make a good first impression and I'm going to make the most of it. The piano wire is in my pocket. It will do me no good in a room full of others. I have to get him alone. Have to win his trust and then get him alone. Already a few are tossing out ideas, nothing too special, everyone wanting to be seen participating, no one willing to say anything that might be held against them at some later date. "People today don't want to be consumers anymore," the one with red hair was explaining, "they want to be in it, part of the game. In a way we need to make them feel like they're part of the company."

"Ideas how to do that," our boss prompts, more jovial and awake than the rest of us put together.

The redhead stands out because of his hair, but so many of the others feel interchangeable, same voices, similar opinions. I should have paid more attention when they were introducing themselves. I stand out and am struggling to own it, take charge of my difference, how I can use it to my advantage. I don't look the same, don't have their false confidence, haven't landed here through normal channels.

"Those scams where the customer can choose the colour of their own car, they're not enough" one of the suits is saying. I notice our boss flinch at the word 'scam.' He doesn't like it, that isn't his particular brand of cynicism. His is more jubilant, more opportunist, about what you can grab, never denigrating the people you have to grab it from. I don't think anyone else notices the flinch as the scam-guy continues: "They need to feel involved, implicated in decisions from day one."

Redhead interrupts: "People have less money, they're nervous to make purchases, credit no longer reassures them. It's like the sweet spot is getting smaller. Every purchase has to feel like the right one, handmade just for them."

Scam-guy: "I don't think that's enough. That's just a glorified version of the right shade of automobile orange. It's like if you ask people: do you want your corporation to be more environmentally responsible? Everyone will say yes. But how to make each person feel that their 'yes' counts, that theirs is one significant vote in the overall direction of the company. It's not just about one isolated purchase; it's more like being part of a family."

I think back to something Emmett told me. His former boss almost always likes it when someone punctures the air in the room, punctures the pretensions. He likes troublemakers, as long as the trouble isn't too sharply directed at him. I start my sentence without knowing how it will end: "I think we need to say that the consumers are us. There are no consumers, we are the consumers, and we need to think about what we like. For example, I like being treated with respect, but I also like to spar, a good fight. I like to fight, but only when I'm confident my opponent respects me."

Redhead interrupts: "Are you saying we should fight with our customers?"

Me: "Maybe not fight them. But we should feel confident enough to occasionally give them a little shove."

Scam-guy: "We know who our customers are. They're definitely not us. We have boxes of statistics about who they are, what they like, how they like to be spoken to."

I have no idea if it's working, but there is no choice but to charge ahead: "Would you like someone to address you, make decisions about your life, based on statistics? But we don't tell them that part. We hide it, and they can sense that something is hidden. When I say 'we are the consumers' I'm talking about honesty, truth in advertising. People need to eat, need to get around—in cars, on bicycles, buses, whatever. We're all here in this room and need to win the approval of this jerk in order to get ahead." I gesture towards the target and he smiles. I don't think anyone can believe I just called our boss a jerk. I can barely believe it myself. "We need to win his approval in order to further our careers. There are basic needs that we all share, that have nothing to do with statistics."

"That's the worst bullshit I've ever heard," our boss interrupts, silencing me, silencing the room, but still beaming, "but at least it's not boring. And I like this guy," he points at me like I was on display, as if I could be bought and sold like everything else in this world. "The problem is I fucking like this guy. He makes me laugh." He was really smiling now, almost laughing. The others look at each other like he's lost his fucking mind, but they're used to it, as I look at my feet, smiling sheepishly. A plan is little more than one step after the next.

1.

I often wonder what exactly happened in that conference room, what happened as I aimlessly drove to nowhere. I know the facts but miss the nuance. That was the moment when everything might have been lost, but instead was so spontaneously, miraculously won. There was no reason for me to phone Emmett, no reason for him to answer, no reason for him to attempt such an audacious, improbable scam. Except that we were desperate, willing to try anything. Why did the heart attack happen at that precise moment, at the moment we needed it most?

Knowing what will happen next is a kind of death, while days when surprise strikes like a tsunami are the ones that genuinely count. Yet still my thoughts of that night, as I tread back over it, again and again, from time to time, fall short of elation. I was at the wheel of my car, ready to drive forever. Back in the boardroom they were deciding my fate. In some ways, for the first time, I had lost my nerve. I had momentarily lost confidence we would prevail. Often I wonder if I've fully recovered, fully returned to my former energized self. The battle for the company dragged on another three years. They sued us for insider trading and we counter-sued with everything we had. There were so many tedious legal arguments. The fight for the inheritance also became increasingly vicious, especially after the first year, when they finally realized there were no legitimate claims involved, but still could not prove it. I am sure they wanted to kill me, but you don't go to war against masters then complain they are too skilled. All of that was more than exhausting, three years of utter devastation.

There is at least one other book written about the battle for my company—a book that, to my taste, portrays me in an unnecessarily harsh light (of course I'm no angel), in fact a book that I now see almost as slander against me. One particular episode it portrays has always felt inaccurate, claiming I was not well within my rights to begin selling off divisions when I did, since at that moment the future ownership of the organization remained in dispute. For me this accusation raises more questions than it answers. I was fighting for my life, and therefore, as I've already made clear, dirty tricks (legal ones) were certainly not out of the question. But what must be understood is that those divisions would have been shed no matter what, regardless of who ended up holding my position. What difference did it make if I sold or they did? Either way a leaner company was required in response to the new, battle-informed situation. But you can't expect factual accuracy on such intricate legal matters from second-rate, now-divorced, hack-slanderers. (There are two names on the spine of that book and, I believe, at the time they wrote it, they were still married.)

The objection might be raised that in order to pay off their leverage, the first thing the new owners would need to do, upon taking control, is sell off the very divisions I had already sold. So, yes, I made their lives more difficult. What was I supposed to do? Make their lives easier. All is fair in love and hostile takeovers. But for the overall fiscal health of the organization, as well as from a legal standpoint, I did nothing that would not have occurred naturally in all potential scenarios.

There are other lies those now-divorced hacks told about me, fanciful ones, a few that were rather dull. (Perhaps my original impulse for writing this book was to set the record straight, give a more accurate impression of my character.) But I also have to admit that, while from time to time I was offended, I thoroughly enjoyed their version of events, every last page, enjoyed it more than I had any right to. The character they present is certainly not me, though my name appears on virtually every page, but a fictional version that is so in control, so calculating, so able to see ten moves ahead of everyone else in the game. If I actually had been as prescient as they claim, the takeover bid would have never been a threat in the first place (and to read their account there was little chance of it ever actually succeeding). There is pleasure in reading a version of myself I know in my heart could never exist, since mine is not an iron mind coldly calculating every possible option and outcome. Instead I am a businessman who loves excitement, loves tension, loves risk and the unexpected, and just happens to possess an extraordinary, on occasion even miraculous, degree of good luck.

I am also a good judge of character. I hire the best, promote the best of the best, and make sure they are doing their jobs. Emmett had the idea to speak to me on the phone not as if I were myself, but as if I were chairman of the board. But I had the idea to hire Emmett, to promote him and promote him again until he was second only to me. I did not leave him alone in that bargaining-session on purpose. It was no brilliantly calculated move on my part. I am sad to admit I panicked, fled a scene I no longer knew how to handle or control. However, if Emmett had been a less capable individual, perhaps I would have been less inclined to leave him in charge.

That other hack-slander book about the war for my company was a bestseller, and if you are reading this now it is perhaps because you have already read it, and it piqued your curiosity. The battle it recounts was only one chapter in the never-ending saga of my life. If it remains the most known episode, I am the last person able to explain why. A soap opera makes a good headline. And to watch Goliath almost felled by a committee of twenty-odd Davids, almost but not quite, a Goliath who almost loses everything and is saved only by a little guile and a great deal of happenstance—these are the reasons why people still read the Bible for entertainment to this day.

I imagine A, B and C reading these pages. I imagine the chief and second-in-command reading them as well. How angry they will be. How savage and unfair they will find each of my recollections. Of course, our lawyers have read through all of this with infinite patience and diligence, and strongly advised against many of my disclosures, so who knows what style or quantity of lawsuits are still to come. I no longer care. Before my retirement I want to set the record straight. We have lawyers and money to handle litigation. But only the truth—or at least the truth as I see it—can cut through the haze of my still-undecided legacy.

When I think of the night of the heart attack, the night that changed everything, there is always something else I wonder, that haunts me. What if we hadn't fought so hard? What if I had let the company go, headed off to do something else, starting from scratch, starting again. Was I still tough enough to build a new company, up from the ground and into a global player? There is nothing I like more than a challenge. Saving my company was one kind of challenge. But perhaps, in doing so, I avoided another, considerably more difficult one.

2.
Then it was back to the phone. He would call once a week to go over my reports. Some weeks he wouldn't phone at all. Be-

fore he had phoned more often, so the brainstorm session did change something, maybe for the worse. Nonetheless, once I actually had him on the line, I continued to feel an increase in our connection.

—So there's the farmer movie and the missile movie. We'll start with the farm one.

—Haven't seen it yet.

—But you approved the script. You did read that?

—Yeah, I read it. About three years ago.

—First the reviews. Most reviewers found the scientist characters credible.

—That's a good thing, right?

—If you say so. The farmer characters received more mixed reactions. Some reviewers thought they were too naive for taking the seeds in the first place.

—Perfect. Scientists credible. Farmers naive. What about the missile one?

I was listening to the recording at home. Listening to it over and over, wanting to understand. We were talking about movies. The people who watched the movies were looking for entertainment or distraction, but we weren't talking about entertainment, only about something else, about implicit perspectives, hidden meanings. Most of the people who worked to get the movie made probably didn't give such perspectives a second thought: the actors thought only about their characters, the director only about making the story convincing or compelling. But someone within our organization had apparently given notes to someone at the division, letting them know what was expected. Or maybe no notes were given, everyone hired for their respective jobs simply understanding the unspoken rules, the need to emphasize certain aspects over others.

—Not many critics liked the missile movie.

—But it's making money?

—Number two for the third week in a row. Lots of money.

—What irked the critics?

—On the whole I think they just found it a bit flat, dull.

—So building a better missile is dull, business as usual?

—They found the moral universe dull. The rush to get the new weapon ready for battle was only noble. Anyone who objected was ridiculous or pathetic. And one thing they all commented is way too many shots of missiles leaving planes, of missiles sailing through the air, etc.

—As long as war is routine we'll always be able to fight it.

—True.

I said true, but it was spin I hadn't actually thought of before. I wasn't sure he had either. He was just talking off the top of his head, saying anything that came to mind, but I wondered if anyone had a thought along these lines that led to the film being made in the precise way it was. I rolled back and listened to the tape again, listened to the way he said 'as long as war is routine.' Was it a new thought or something he'd already had a thousand times? His voice gave nothing away.

—Anything in the editorials? Did anyone use either film as an example?

—A few. A right-wing paper compared the bad general to the current administration. His conclusion was that those who are against innovation are also against efficiency.

—Left-wing editorials?

—A few in-betweeners. The farm movie was used only as a negative example in the two editorials that mention it. Do you know who Lysenko is?

—Russian scientist. Didn't work out so well for him, right?

—Exactly. One editorial says the film, and the world, have invented another Lysenko, and because the field is now global, the results will be even more tragic.

—An article that mentions some obscure Russian scientist isn't going to get a lot of traction.

—The other in-betweener was more positive. Said science is a process of trial and error, both in the laboratory and out in the world, and there is no mistake so drastic it doesn't teach us something profound. It sounds negative in capsule but the overall feel was pro-science.

I wondered what kind of strange game I was playing, pretending to stand behind my report, pretending to agree with this man I had dedicated my life to wanting to kill. What did I really believe and to what degree did it differ from the things I listened to myself saying over and over again on these recordings? Did I care what some asshole working for a substandard right-wing broadsheet in the middle of nowhere said about a mediocre pseudo-fascist war movie? There were a million opinions in the world, and if you searched hard enough you could find someone willing to take up every single slot along the spectrum of possible positions. With money you could spread the mania of your particular view, and in spreading it also make it seem more true. But anyone with open eyes can look at the world and see what is what. What movies are garbage and whose agenda they are not so subtly pushing.

However, in any circumstances it would most likely feel strange to perpetually express the opposite of what one thinks and feels, week after week, and this fact must have been at the root of my growing anxiety that over time my thoughts were falling in line with my words.

—Did anyone connect the movie with the civilian bombings?

—I didn't find much. That's actually strange, isn't it? The

movie came out the same week the bombings were front-page news.

—The studio wanted to postpone the release, but I thought it would be okay. Sometimes these things are so obvious everyone just misses them. If the movie was released a few weeks later it might have given a few astute journalists enough time to figure it out.

—If you find a few astute journalists let me know.

—There must still be a few out there somewhere.

—So I guess timing is everything?

—Money is everything. Timing is just a bit of good luck when you need it most.

1.

The other thing about poetry is I lead an extremely busy life. It only takes a few minutes to read a poem. I read one or two a night just before falling asleep. Often they put me to sleep, which during stressful periods can be extremely useful. Just as often they stimulate my dreams. Dreams are important in business. All clichés are important in business, but for me personally my dreams have, on many occasions, shown me the way forward in particularly knotty or difficult situations. After the night of the heart attack, there was one such situation along with a corresponding dream. One of the many tactics the other side unleashed upon us was a government investigation. In confiscating Emmett's cell phone, a manoeuvre the legality of which still feels suspect to me, one particularly clever government official was able to discover Emmett's ruse, that he did not in fact phone any members of the board that night, that he only phoned me as I aimlessly drove, and therefore we had been bargaining in bad faith. Whether or not our spontaneous play-acting was factually illegal is beside the point. We were under investigation and they were working hard to make any charge stick.

The night before I went to give my statement, I had the following dream. I had not read any poems before going to bed, which the next morning only added to my conviction that the dream had begun in some deep place within me. Emmett and I were at war with each other, fighting for separate armies, separate countries. We were not generals—often I'm a general or president in my dreams—but foot soldiers, nobodies. Strangely, in the dream I did not know Emmett, had never met him, had no idea who he was. The battlefield was a barely discernable mix of history and fiction, of two World Wars, guerrilla wars, wars from movies, books and comics. I was running and shooting but had somehow gotten turned around, there was smoke or maybe poisonous gas filling the landscape, I wasn't sure which way to run, which way was toward enemy lines and whether I wanted to charge towards them or retreat. I tripped, rolled headfirst, and when I managed to find my feet I was in some sort of trench, up to my waist in freezing water, pushing through it, not sure if I would be physically able to climb back out. It was difficult to see even a few feet ahead, and when my face hit something, it wasn't clear what it was, my eyes still adjusting to the cinematic light. Because it was a dream, one moment I had no idea what was in front of me and the next moment realized it was Emmett, a complete stranger, an enemy, that I had stumbled directly into the barrel of his loaded rifle. I looked straight at him. I wanted my eyes to convey that I could take him, that we were evenly matched. I wanted my eyes to strike fear into him even though he had the clear, even overwhelming, advantage. And then we were both under attack. The charge came from the other side. He was the only thing standing between me and the advancing soldiers. He took the bullets first as I awoke.

In business, the most profitable situation is always a pure monopoly. Monopolies are difficult to maintain and, over time, become increasingly dull to operate. As everyone knows, I prefer excitement. But I am a businessman and therefore the drive towards monopoly is in my blood. There is a considerable degree of governmental regulation against the forming of monopolies. But regulations require definitions, and in the real world definitions are always slippery. The legal framework for the various divisions within our organization is a constant source of negotiation. To what extent are the divisions interlinked parts of a single organization, and to what extent are they autonomous entities? In a strictly legal sense, these questions spread out infinitely in every direction. So while there is often speculation as to whether or not we are, statistically speaking, the single largest corporation in the world at any given time, I always insist that I do not consider our undertaking in these terms. I continue to think of us as a series of smaller, vibrant families that struggle to fully embody our common interests and drives.

We endlessly discussed how to proceed with Emmett's ongoing role in the organization. Much of this debate took place in the years directly following his indictment. I was certain we could find a low-profile position for him within one of the safer divisions—far away from the most profitable, and controversial, core businesses—where he could relax for a few years until the optics of his situation grew more calm. Sadly, this was not how events played out, and in my more reflective moments I find myself wondering why our friendship had to suffer through what, to me, felt like eminently manageable, one might even say run-of-the-mill, corporate legal duress. Friendship is built on trust and, from my side of the equation, I trusted Emmett forever. But apparently this 'forever' was not mutual and, to my deep dismay, things went from bad to worse.

The more I have lived in the business world, the more I've come to believe that the drive towards monopoly contains within it what one might call a spiritual component. You want to take all the separate parts and make them whole again, unite them into one single entity. The desire for wholeness is little more than a desire for cohesion, the desire for things and people to work smoothly together rather than being at odds. Over the years, many have criticized the way our organization treated Emmett, but I have always tried to live without regrets. When you take chances, you invite scandal. Emmett fared worse in the investigation than many of our other employees, and the fact that he knew so many of the details that I personally had no knowledge of did not work to his overall advantage. He could joke his way out of anything but, in the end, could not joke his way out of everything. Nonetheless, he will always remain my favourite and my friend.

2.
Sometimes, around the end of the day, I aimlessly wander the building, hoping to accidentally encounter my target. I wander through hallway after hallway, reading the names on the doors, riding the elevators all the way to the top and back down to the parking lot. Emmett had shown me how to unlock my pass, so I can wander freely, saying hello to workers as they walk by, listening to their hesitant replies, unsure whether or not they had met me before. Security outside the

building was tight, but once you were in, once you were gainfully employed, things were considerably more relaxed. A few times each evening I would see a security guard, who would glance down at my pass and then smile like the rest. The building was a sad, dull place. A place where people come to sate their misplaced ambition, or collect a pay cheque, thinking little more of it. A place where actions have only unexamined consequences. When the halls were empty you could feel the degree to which nothing lived here. Only work and stress, little real life. Ambitions galore but so few human desires. As I wandered I would think what it meant for me to have this job. I come here every day and do not mean any of it. It is a lie, an impersonation, a means to an end. How many people worked not in order to do the tasks they were actually doing, but instead only for the pay cheque or status. So many things were not what they actually were, not for their own sake, but means to various ends, some more noble, some less.

I step into the elevator and press the button down to the parking lot. I don't have a car but, before heading home, thought I would wander through all the vehicles. Think about oil and status, who had already gone home and who was still here, working late. Instead of going down, the elevator first goes up, stops at a floor near the top. He gets in and smiles at me. It is a moment before I say hello, and when I do I can feel the recognition kick in. He still recognizes my voice far more than my face. We still go over my reports on the phone almost every week. He doesn't remember my name and I don't help him. Let us both stand here in the awkwardness for as long as possible. I realize I am no one to him, just another employee among millions. A moment later I have the piano wire around his neck and I'm tightening with every ounce of strength. It's like riding a bull the way he smashes me against one wall, then the next, takes everything I have to just hold on. I am strangling him, can feel his breath leaving, yet it also feels like he has the upper hand. He's at least twenty years older but maybe also twice as strong. Somehow he gets a few fingers under my wire, so it no longer entirely connects with his neck, as he smashes me against the elevator buttons and the doors open at some random floor. We are struggling out into the hallway. I'm pulling, he's getting weaker, but I still don't have him. I feel his teeth sinking into my wrist and I'm bleeding. Five, six times he smashes me into the wall, I can't believe how hard, his teeth tearing into my other wrist. I swear I only let up for a millisecond, but it's enough for him to break free. He collapses on the ground in front of me as I collapse back against the wall. We're both exhausted and he's not dead. His face is completely covered in my blood. So is my suit. He looks at me, gasping for breath, finding his words. He can see that I'm also spent so he takes his time, says he should probably call security but if I leave now, never come back, he'll let me go. No questions asked. He doesn't want the trouble of an investigation. In the way he says all this there is something strange, elated, as if he was excited to realize he still has so much fight left in him, that he still wants to live so viciously. I nod yes as he struggles to get back up, find his bearings. The moment he turns his back I once again charge. I don't know what I'm thinking, have no plan, only rage. I have wanted this for so long, there is no way I can fail. To come so close and then fall short would be worse than death.

I no longer have the piano wire but, since his throat is already weakened, instinctively continue at his neck. He smashes me in the head before I manage to get my arm around him, some sort of awkward chokehold, struggling to get a firmer grip, but now it's no use. He shed me once and he's confident he can do it again, fingers in my eyes, fist smashing against my teeth too fast for me to bite and I lose my grip, my foot connecting with his stomach only once, with every ounce of my strength, before he has me by the ankle and I'm on the ground in front of him. Then a security guard rounds the corner and it's done.

Only a few hours later I'm on a bus, all the money I have in an elastic band in my pocket. Once they had me in handcuffs, which a security guard first had to go fetch, the bastard again repeated his spiel about letting me go with no questions asked. He didn't know why I wanted him dead, but there were lots of people who wanted him dead, for all sorts of reasons, many of them valid. As he was telling me this he was wiping the blood off his face and hands with an endless series of handy wipes from a box another guard also had to go get. At one moment he thinks to offer me one, then realizes my hands are cuffed behind my back and thinks better of it. He's regaining his composure as he speaks. It's like I've barely fazed him. And as he calmly explains that if I am ever seen in his vicinity again he will have no choice but to send me to jail—the kind of jail where you disappear forever, where they put a bag over your head and place you in infinite amounts of pain—I start to shake and then start to cry. I am not crying because I'm afraid of torture. I'm crying because I have failed so completely and I can't stop, sobbing more and more violently. If he has the ability to send me off to some secret prison why doesn't he do so now, why let me go, why take the risk. Because he wants to humiliate me, show me I'm no real threat, that he can take me any time, that he's not afraid. He says maybe I did this because I wanted to become famous, but he's not going to let it go public, not going to make me famous. He's simply sending me away and I'll disappear, remain as anonymous as I've always been. In a moment I'll be gone like nothing had even happened.

94

On the bus I stare at my wrists, which I've hastily bandaged with some gauze and tape. I look like a suicide attempt. If others here look at me, that's most likely what they think. I barely even know which way the bus is headed. I did ask when I got on, and learned the journey lasts fourteen hours. I wonder if I'm in too much pain to sleep, look down at the dirty white gauze lying limp in my lap, and my phone rings. It's Emmett. He begins to explain that he has a plan, a plan he's been working on for many years, and he needs my help. He has commissioned a computer virus and I'm the only one who can insert it into the system. The procedure will be extremely similar to the one I used to break open my pass. If everything goes well, and if I agree, he believes my actions could destroy the company almost entirely, or at the very least force the board to fire our target, replace him in their panicked search to curtail the disintegration. He goes on to carefully explain detail after detail, completely oblivious to the enormity of his bad timing as, once again, I begin to cry.

Part 2

1.

I had hired a detective to trace his history, find out who he was and why he had attacked me. It was then I learned that Emmett had also hired a detective, from the same agency, the agency we most often use. We had both hired practically the same detective to find out about the same man, only Emmett had done so two years before me. How did they know each other? How does a concert pianist turned under-the-table dishwasher possibly meet an Ivy League operator like Emmett? I still have no fucking idea.

At first I spoke openly about the attack, laughed it off, said it reminded me of my days fighting other kids on the block, that I missed those days, was still up for a good rumble when the opportunity arose. But when I joked the reactions were rarely jovial. I realized there must be rumours. Who would want to attack me and why? Other companies looking to gain an edge? People I'd fucked over, former employees? My suspicion was this: as they speculated on where the attack originated, they simultaneously realized just how many people in the world had reason to desire my injury or death. Then it was no longer funny. It was as if there must be something wrong with me if I had so many enemies, had pissed off so many different kinds of people. I was tainted. If, off the top of your head, an endless list of possible avengers leap to mind, does that still leave me as a valid option? What evidence is there that I'm the one who should keep running the show? So I stopped mentioning the attack and no one else mentioned it either. And yet I could feel it was still in the air, worried I was becoming paranoid or, worse, that something had actually changed.

I still haven't told anyone about the connection between the attack and Emmett. Everyone liked Emmett, and if they had to choose between me and him, who knows. Even I liked Emmett. For years after he left, I barely thought of him; it was as if I had thrown him out of my mind, and now I find myself thinking about him constantly, every day. What is the connection?

2.

I get off the bus and find a cheap hotel near the station. I lie on the bed with all the lights on, staring at the ceiling. My life is over. I have failed. I sit up, reach into my pocket, peel the elastic band from the slightly damp bills. My calculations are rough, but I think it might be enough to last about six months. It is everything I earned working for the people I hate, and the idea of spending it makes me feel absolutely sick. But there's no point putting money in the garbage, and my disgust will certainly not aid me in making good decisions. Will I go back to washing dishes? Can I possibly stomach the idea of teaching children to play piano? Are there even children, or parents, who still care enough about playing classical piano these days that they are willing to pay someone properly to instruct them? I lie back down and instantly fall asleep. I don't know how long I sleep, have no dreams, or none I can remember, and am awoken by the maid loudly knocking at the door. I yell that I'm still sleeping and she goes away. I believe she apologizes first but can't quite hear her. I haven't yelled at anyone in years, and fear my voice sounded angrier than I meant. The maid clearly doesn't deserve my rage. And those who do are already far away.

I prop my head up on some pillows and slowly look around the room. There is nothing pleasing about it. It's plain and worn down. It looks how I feel. The curtain is directly next to the bed and I draw it back. Sunlight streams past me, making the room look both brighter and worse. I have travelled here to nowhere, worried that if I stayed where I was, the bastard would have changed his mind and thrown me in jail. A few of the security guards had escorted me back to my apartment to gather up my belongings, to the drug store to buy gauze for my wrists, to the bank to withdraw whatever I had left and close my account, and finally to the train station. They did all of this with meticulous calm. They had their instructions and carefully guided me through each step. And the entire time I felt that if I had done anything out of line, even if I had made the wrong sudden movement, they would have killed me on the spot.

I go to the bathroom and shower, taking extra care to clean my damaged wrists, cleaning them carefully and then cleaning them again, as if they had been bitten by someone rabid. When I get out of the shower I take new gauze and re-bandage. As I do so, I think again about suicide. Is that the price for absolute failure? Could anything possibly happen in my life now that would redeem me? I also think about writing a book, my own autobiography, that would explain to the world everything that had happened and why. But who would publish such a book? Even to begin thinking about it seems impossible. I feel especially interested in writing about my time working for the people I hate. To reveal some of the hidden daily corruptions that lie just a few inches behind their advertised good image. But there are millions of books published every year exposing the world's corruption, and the corruption of the world only increases. Each book, in its own way, has teeth but nothing to bite into. No clear way to attack. There are also millions of books each year pushing for things to remain the same, or teaching you how to make money at the expense of others. Everything balances out, but the balance is so deeply imperfect, always tilting further and further towards the worst.

Of course there is no point thinking this way, I try to tell myself as I step out into the much too dusty street and sunlight. You only think these things because your one and only plan was an overwhelming failure and this fact has affected your mood. I had asked at the counter which way was downtown, and find myself slowly walking in that direction.

1.
Today I did something strange: I re-read my own autobiography. Unsurprisingly, it was a fast read. I finished almost the entire thing on a single flight. So many aspects within it surprised me, incidents I had forgotten or that didn't happen quite the way I recounted them. I am now trying to recall exactly why I agreed to write it in the first place. Why was I so forthcoming, so elaborate? I know myself, that I care what others think far more than anyone might suspect or realize. That I care about stupidities such as legacy. When I meet new people, I sometimes feel I can tell whether or not they've read the book by the way they treat me. Those who haven't read

it are easier to charm, while those who have are slightly on edge, almost suspicious. When I started the book I was convinced it was time to retire, but now, as they gracefully try to ease me out, push me towards a more symbolic leadership position, it seems I once again want to fight, hang on just a few more years.

The press release calls it an 'extensive research trip,' but I now realize it is something much closer to probation. I am travelling for work, having meetings, seeing many of our operations around the world. But back at home my decisions are no longer acted upon with lightning speed. I am still in charge, yet not in charge to anywhere near the degree I once was. But is this actually the case? Of course no one will look me in the eye and tell me so, that anything has changed. Instead they tell me to keep travelling. This trip was originally my idea, my decision. I thought it would be good to get some perspective on the overall scope of our organization. But when I boarded that first airplane, it seems I also showed my throat.

In Germany, I am in a meeting with several executives from what was once a local media group consisting of forty television and radio stations. They are somewhat less than thrilled to be meeting with me, fearful that my visit equals imminent cutbacks. I assure them I'm only here on a sightseeing tour, but they seem unconvinced. When I use words like 'creativity' or 'vision' they bristle. I can feel that this is not the way they do things. They prefer careful research and planning. I change tack, expressing somewhat less-than-genuine interest in their lengthy statistics and projections, how they hope to slowly dominate the national market over the next twenty years. I casually mention that I look forward to seeing their plans come true and, as I do so, one of them, I think he might be the youngest—it is a family business, so perhaps he's even the grandson or great-grandson of the original founder—looks straight at me with a look I can't quite decipher. I ask him if anything is wrong and his answer bothers me all the way back to the hotel. He says, less than tactfully he later admits, that no, it's nothing. He just can't imagine I'll still be around in twenty years. It was just a strange thought for him.

2.

The downtown strips of small towns like these are endlessly alike. I have only been to a few in my life and yet, in my memory, can barely tell them apart, nor can I tell any of them apart from the one I currently find myself in. I am looking at the street, at the storefronts, and thinking of what I did wrong. The piano wire was too nostalgic, too ineffective. A knife or gun would have been better. I am wondering if there is any way I can go back, try again, or convince someone else to go in my place. Or if there's another billionaire I could train my sights on, turning the first attempt into a test run. What if I tell myself it had only been a chance to try things out, to carefully learn from my mistakes. I can feel the roll of bills in my pocket and wonder if I should buy anything, new clothes that would be as inconspicuous as possible. I am back in my dishwasher's attire, having left the suits, anything that was expensive, far behind.

I am about to go into a diner for cheap coffee when I see something ahead, at the very end of the road. It's a lot of people, they look almost like a mirage, since they are far away in the heat. With nothing else to do in life, since I don't even know why I'm here, I start walking towards them, and it is a few long minutes before I realize it's a much larger crowd, they are much further away, than I originally thought. By the time I reach them I'm sweating hard, the sun here is cruel, and I've arrived at the far edge of town, which opens out towards a field, though there is more dirt than grass. In front of me are maybe a few thousand people doing nothing. I stand at the edge of the crowd gazing into it, thinking that I have no idea where I am or what I'm looking at. A small cluster of men stand directly in front of me, and I begin to eavesdrop. Only moments later do I realize that they're speaking my language, the language from childhood. I hear it so rarely now that sometimes I almost forget. A part of me must believe I have left that language behind forever, but here it is again, directly in front of me, like a message from the past.

One of the men sees me, realizes I am listening, calls me over. As I walk towards him, I wonder if I will still remember how to speak.

Him: You looking for work too?
Me: That's what we're all doing here? Looking for work?
Him: What else?
Me: How long have you been waiting?
Him: A couple of days.
Me: I just got here.
Him: Obviously. What do we look like, a bunch of fucking idiots?

He laughs, but warmly, and his friends laugh along with him. I feel I'm speaking like a child, or not quite like a child but definitely not like myself. Perhaps only like my younger self. At the same time, as I speak, more and more words come back to me, flooding back into my head.

I spend the afternoon with them, learning how it all works, amazed at how open and relaxed they become with me, maybe only because we're speaking the same words and therefore they consider me family. You wait here in the field and a bus pulls up. A man gets out of the bus and announces the crop: oranges, cucumbers, soy, etc. Everyone scurries towards the bus and they count off the heads as people scramble on. The moment the bus is full it drives away. In the morning, often there are several buses for each crop. As it moves towards noon things slow down considerably until finally, around one, there are no more buses, and those left behind have to wait until tomorrow. When the sun goes down the buses return, drop everyone back here, and people cook, set up tents, drink, or just try to find sleep on some patch of dirt, hopeful for a more lucrative day tomorrow. The work is hard and the pay meagre, 'like the dirt we're all standing on,' they joke, but if you're lucky you can save a little to take home when the season is done.

What is clear is that the guys I'm talking to—and most of those who surround us, who practically litter this field, scattered haphazardly in every direction—must, each in their own way, feel they have no choice. Being here clearly sucks, standing around like some crappy products on a supermarket shelf that the buses can scoop up or leave behind, it makes little difference. Whatever awaits them back home is likely far worse. Actually, they don't speak much to me about home, which is perhaps why I assume the worst.

The next morning, first thing, I find myself back at the edge of the same field. I have no desire to farm, but it feels good to speak my own language, a reminder of life before the piano, of long before one single-minded, murderous goal consumed the totality of my days. Maybe farming is good honest work, maybe I now need something honest in my life, but from the way I stand here, from the feelings I am sure are splashed across my face in Technicolor, I remain unconvinced. I slowly shuffle through the crowd, finding my friends from the day before. They receive me warmly and I think about how long its been since anyone has greeted me with genuine warmth. Is it possible the last time was when I was a child? And then, without me quite realizing what has happened, they all rush towards a bus that just arrived and, pushed forward by the crowd, I rush along with them, hesitating for a brief moment before I climb on, as others shove past me and the bus pulls away. They wave to me from the window, laughing, telling jokes to each other (or at least so it seems) about what a rank amateur I am, and how stupid I must look standing there alone as the bus recedes into the distance.

1.

What could I still do that would genuinely surprise? That would jolt those who had lost faith in me, pull the carpet out from under their preconceptions, force them to see me in a different light? One event directly preceded my current, endless travel: the global market crash and the rather banal subsequent bailout. I've lived through a few big crashes in my life, but this was by far the most apocalyptic. I think few people to this day realize the actual, overwhelming extent of it. Maybe it had something to do with the attack, from which I was still recovering, but it takes a lot to shake me and I was shaken. This was back when I was drinking, so it was alcohol I'd most often make use of to calm my nerves. I was in the bar, around noon, when the calamity was first announced, and a few dozen of us leapt out of our chairs, hurrying back to our respective offices, but on my way to the front door I realized the bar was a considerably more attractive proposal, and as I looked around it was clear that half the room was panicking, rushing to work, while the other half was calm.

I was carefully scanning the room, or at least as carefully as I could considering I'd already had quite a bit to drink, making a mental note of each face, but mainly focusing on those who seemed a bit too relaxed, who were taking the whole thing in stride. These were not poker faces, I remember thinking at the time, not some calm exterior covering up a world of inner turmoil. These were people utterly convinced that, when all was said and done, they would come out ahead, in fact convinced the crash was the best possible thing that could happen to them, that when everything is given a good shake, some people lose while others take, each and every one of them certain they would be the one taking the most.

I was memorizing each of their faces because I wanted to know, to check later, when things had calmed down, whether each of these men were overconfident or accurate in their predictions. When I got back to the office I made a list, wrote down each of the names I could remember and left it on my desk, glancing down at it every few days as the chaos swirled around me, as we debated which divisions to sell off and if there were any that had to be shut down altogether. We came out the other end okay, but I realized so many others had done better, seized the opportunity more fully. A crash is a chance to expand, and yet we shrank ever so slightly, telling me I had done something wrong, hadn't been fast enough.

And then I would look at the list on my desk. Almost every

name on it had done better than me. Had they been prepared from the start? Or anticipated the calamity before me? Had the attack shaken my instincts, distracted me, made me less effective at the very moment the organization needed me most? Was I simply drinking too much? Or drinking too much in direct response to the attack? Then there was the question of who got how much in bailout cash. We lobbied with calm determination but so many others got more. And yet, since everyone knew the official numbers were nowhere close to reality, the question of who got what was an endless source of speculation. I heard a rumour that we got twice as much as everyone else put together. This is clearly untrue and strikes me as verging on slander. We did poorly in the shakedown and then, behind our backs, people were saying we did twice as well. I couldn't think of any of this without fearing, almost to the point of panic, that I had lost my touch. In some ways, I became obsessed with these men who came out the other side far richer than they went in. It was unlike me to obsess over other people's business. In the past I'd always remained productively, almost myopically, focused on my own, on the task at hand. This was a change for the worse.

2.
I went to the field every day, never quite working up the courage to climb onto a bus, and though in many ways being here calmed me, when I thought about recent events, or about coming here, or about anything, mainly I felt depressed, or worse than depressed, devastated. So I tried not to think and instead only to listen, throwing my energy into what I might learn from these people I would most likely never see again. I talked to worker after worker, from different countries, differ-

ent worlds, all here to make some cash then drift back home. And the more we spoke, the more I listened, the more I became obsessed with the word 'pesticides,' since symptoms and illnesses kept being mentioned. They would show me rashes on their hands, face or neck, demonstrate a rasping cough that wouldn't go away, or ask me to look into their eyes, often red and irritated, worry in their voices that if they kept going perhaps they'd end up half-blind.

I thought about food and poison, how strange it was to find them together in field after field, crop after crop. This society, this culture, has a death wish, I thought as I listened to these illness stories. (My mind had a particularly dark cast at that time.) A death wish that takes the form of cancer, of workers whose lives are shortened by their work, of hiding the elderly away in homes where no one can see them. What we don't want to look at, we think we don't have to deal with, and then it owns us completely. Cancers from the food we eat and the water we drink, from the computers under our fingers and the cell phones pressed against our heads. What is cancer but cells that will not stop growing, infinite growth in a finite world? I wasn't thinking straight, unhinged by the delirium of recent events, but it did seem reasonable to me that harvesting fruits and vegetables shouldn't make you feel sick.

But poison wasn't the only, or even main problem here. These people were expendable and they knew it. They needed the money but the employers didn't need them. The field held an endless supply of workers, the buses came and went, filled and emptied. Whoever could get to the bus first would win the salary for that shift, depending on how much they could get into their basket, yet it all seemed as arbitrary as a storm. I liked these people, liked coming to talk to them every day, how they were completely lost, with no hope but much time, or at least they had a great deal of time if they weren't one of the lucky ones to make it onto the bus on that particular day. And I was also completely lost. I had slightly more options than these workers, but definitely not more hope. There wasn't much food and almost no alcohol, but what they had, they shared. I was probably idealizing them far too much. But here in the encampment I just couldn't be critical, couldn't think anything bad about them. It felt so much better here than anything I had left behind.

One night, as I was walking home, my phone rang. I had forgotten I even had a phone in my pocket, and was surprised it still worked. On the other end of the line I found Emmett. He wanted to know if I had inserted the virus into the system yet. I realized that when I had last spoken to him, on the bus, I'd been too drained, too depleted, to explain what had happened, to explain that I no longer worked there. Now, slowly, getting lost several times along the way, I tried to explain everything: the piano wire, the elevator, my wrists, the gauze, the bus, the field. It took a while before he fully understood, and then he was furious. As I slowly walked back towards the hotel, he yelled at me for at least an hour. I had never before been on the receiving end of such anger and vitriol. He'd had a foolproof plan to bring down the entire organization, and I'd squandered it on some paltry, piano wire attempt to bring down just one man.

I had no idea why I didn't hang up on him. For some reason I wanted to hear what he had to say, take his lashes and see what happened. He was now attacking me the same way as, back when he worked for them, he had once attacked the world. He yelled at me like he wanted me dead, like with every word, every insult, he wanted to kill me. And I thought how power-less he had become, yelling at me as I strolled home through the gentle twilight, how there was a time in his life when he would say things, give orders, and people might actually end up dead or injured—for example, workers trying to unionize in some far-off backwater, much like where I grew up—and now he had nothing better to do with his time than yell at me, someone even more powerless than he was. He was calling me a shit-assed idiot cocksucker and for some reason I started laughing. It seemed so ridiculous, his furious yelling and the fact that it all felt so far away, a hundred lifetimes ago, that now I basically couldn't care less. I interrupted him.

Me: You waited too long. You should have confided in me sooner.
Him: What?
Me: If you wanted me as an ally, if you wanted my help, you had to bring me on board sooner. I didn't know. I had my own plan and it seemed good enough at the time. I didn't know about your plan. You can't have allies if you keep them in the dark.

There was silence on the other end of the line. I thought he had tired himself out, that he had nothing left. It was a long si-lence but I didn't hang up. I kept the phone pressed against my ear, listening to nothing, wondering who would hang up first.

1.
I'm not sure how or when the notion that Emmett was en-tertaining—that he was the constant life of the party—first arose, but it was certainly repeated frequently enough over

the years. Perhaps it began only as a sarcastic comment that someone without a good ear for sarcasm took too literally. I am also not sure why, when I began writing the book, I thought it would be a comical myth to perpetuate. Pretending the most humourless, mean-hearted, legal pit bull I have ever had the pleasure of knowing was instead a laugh-a-minute joke machine just felt right to me at the time, like a lie that concealed some greater truth, though with the considerable benefit of hindsight, I can no longer intuit what that greater truth might have been.

Emmett was our dirty jobs expert, perfect at going in for the kill, and therefore there was something perverse and poetic in painting him in this lighter hue. Many within our organization had heard frequent rumours of how entertaining he was, and were often shocked to finally meet him in person, perhaps assuming they had simply caught him on a bad day. But what was true is that he was the closest friend I'd ever had within the organization, and when he turned on me it was as if something broke. The fact that he was somehow tangled up in the attack, with that shithead in the elevator wrapping wire around my neck, is by far the most disturbing aspect of the entire incident. I want to give a name to my would-be killer. What should I call him? Something that will ease his presence in my mind, make him look foolish, like he is of no threat and never was, which is in fact the truth. I don't want his real name, which is meaningless to me, but instead something I control, something I own, some way to own that piano-idiot who attacked me.

There is a frequent pattern to my experiences in foreign cities. I arrive and am picked up at the airport by a junior employee, who first takes me to drop off my bags at the hotel. In the car, as we drive, I often ask questions about the company. With the inexperienced, it's sometimes possible to get honest answers simply by asking direct questions at the exact moment they are least expecting it. In Italy, I am picked up at the airport by a young man who couldn't have been more than twenty. He was an especially interesting case. When asked about his division, he would give roundabout answers, speaking about things I did not at first understand, though he spoke clearly enough and was never less than intriguing. He said that everyone who worked for his company was a virtuoso, because all workers today are expected to be virtuosos. A virtuoso was someone who could do many different jobs well, who could slide from one to the next with natural ease. And because working life for his generation was precarious, far more precarious than anything my generation had ever known, they had to be virtuosos. They would each have many different, many different kinds, of jobs in their lifetime. They had to be able to do each of them well, to retrain quickly, to think and learn on their feet. His English was definitely not perfect, and I wondered why he was telling me all this. It was like he had already decided I was old-fashioned, that I didn't understand how the world worked today, and wanted to set me straight.

But of course, because he wanted to set me straight, I also wanted to set him straight, show him which of us was the voice of expertise and experience. Did he have any idea how many different jobs I'd had in my storied life, how many different kinds of businesses I had expertly run to get where I was today? Did he think his was the first generation to display flexibility? Because every generation thinks they're different, unique, have reinvented everything that came before. My generation also thought we had reinvented the wheel and were creating something unprecedented. But things don't change so much. In the end, his generation, much like my own, would realize they were repeating so many of the patterns that had come before. And he would realize it much like I was realizing it now, when someday someone much younger than him presented things he already knew all too well, and yet presented them as the brand new, exciting wave of the future. Then I told him that what was even a little tragic about what he was telling me is that it might be another twenty, thirty, forty years before he fully realizes, fully feels, how what he is saying now is genuinely not the full historical truth of his situation.

After my rant he took a long pause, as if he was carefully thinking over what I had said, which pleased me in spite of myself, and when he began speaking again he chose his words with much greater care. The difference, he explained, between his generation and mine is that his generation would use their virtuosity to undo business, the way businesses are run, and then put them back together using a far more collaborative model, with a more equal distribution of profits. They were virtuosos of collaboration and therefore had the skills to do so. It was like he thought he and his friends had invented Marx, and I wondered if maybe they could use their virtuosity to invent the Bible while they were at it. Then he told me that possibly I thought business, in its current form, would last forever, but I should look at my historical knowledge, since it would teach me that nothing lasts forever, everything changes, and while most often things change for the worse, if we work hard maybe sometimes things might also change for the better. And then he said something that really landed with me. He told me that he used the word 'we' on purpose, because he didn't know me yet and therefore didn't want to assume anything, didn't want to assume I was the enemy. It seemed unlikely to him, but maybe if we talked, if he explained things to me as we drove from the airport to the hotel, I too might begin to think about the world differently and become part of the 'we' that is working, utilizing my own brand of virtuosity, towards something better. He wasn't naive, but for him being too cynical was a kind of death, so he would prefer to see some sliver of possibility in every situation that presents itself, no matter how unlikely, which is why he volunteered to pick me up at the airport in the first place.

As I was unpacking my suitcase, hanging my suits one by one in the closet, I thought about how much harder the future would be than the immediate past. I wasn't born rich—I struggled and improbably made it—but in the future, more and more, people would be rich only because they were born into it. It did not seem to me that my story was a template that would continue to repeat. They, the virtuosos of the future, were virtuosos with considerably less opportunity. Opportunities are short-lived. They last a few generations and then, victims of their own success, shut down again, as assholes like me close rank. So I understood why that young man wanted to reinvent business. The way it was currently organized would not serve his interests towards the same glory that it had once served mine. And then for a brief moment, in a different way than I had understood it before, I thought I understood why someone might want to attack me, why someone from the next generation might want me dead.

2.
Then one day, without knowing quite how it happened, I was on a bus, on my way to harvest tomatoes. So many days I had watched others pile onto the buses and not gotten on myself.

Perhaps it was only that I was starting to feel like a tourist, but also my new friends were teasing me more and more mercilessly. I was the loser who never managed to make it onto a bus, the comical one who never managed to make a cent. I tried to take their jibes with good humour, because of course I knew what they did not, that I hadn't come here to work and my money had not yet run out. But I didn't like being teased. I wanted their respect.

But again that's not precisely how it happened. There was a rush towards a bus and moments later I was seated inside as the bus pulled away. It was early, some time around dawn, and I'd been up all night talking and laughing. I really did like these people, and now I was going to see for myself what a day of work consisted of for them. The bus ride lasted just less than an hour. We were herded off the bus and suddenly everyone was running, rushing to get the best spots. For some reason I don't rush, and end up with a spot furthest away from where the bus drops us off. As I start to work, carefully observing those around me to see how it is done, it becomes clear why mine is a spot no one else wants. It's in the shade, where the tomatoes are noticeably less ripe, smaller. I have to search to find ones ready to pick. But what's worse is I am farthest away from the bins, have to drag my cart across the entirety of the field to have it weighed and receive a token. The cart can barely roll and frequently gets stuck in the mud. I manage to fill it only a few times, and on each of these occasions the time I lose dragging it would have been enough for a more experienced worker to fill it over and over again. At the end of the day you turn in the tokens for cash. Before they give you the cash they deduct the cost of the bus ride, the water you drunk while working in the heat, the meagre lunch I wolfed down in half a minute between trips out to the far side of the field. For most of the others here they're also deducting the cost of being smuggled over the border, deducting it in daily instalments that seem exorbitant, ridiculous. When we're done I have only a few tokens and, after the deductions, there's nothing left. If I was hoping to earn the respect of my fellow workers, I have failed. Even the worst of them managed to pick ten times as much as me. My eyes, hands, mouth, teeth and throat are all irritated from the pesticides. My arms and shoulders ache from picking. My back aches from dragging the cart through the dirt. I am so exhausted I can barely stand.

Back at the encampment, as we pass around a bottle of homemade stuff I should recognize from my teenage years back home but for some reason don't, the others laugh at me as I tell them about my first day. Some are laughing so hard they can barely remain upright. I realize the story is funnier because I still don't speak properly. So much of the language has come back but I still miss words, expressing myself awkwardly, getting the expressions wrong. I feel frustrated I can't put things right, place my words correctly, but even though I'm embarrassed and don't particularly enjoy being the object of ridicule, I'm nonetheless happy to be entertaining my new friends. Maybe I'm wrong, but it feels they're laughing at me in a way that only friends can laugh at each other. Then one of them suddenly stops laughing. He's had a thought, a new question, struck by how obvious this new thought now seems to him. He wants to know why, if I don't farm, if I've never harvested, I mean, what the fuck am I doing here? It makes no sense. No one comes to a place like this just to hang out. Or to make new friends.

I wonder if I should tell them the whole story: pianos, shareholder reports, bonfires, billionaires, elevators and gauze. I do want to tell someone. Having this story inside of me, that no one knows except Emmett, and not even he knows the entire thing, is like acid in my stomach. I feel that telling someone, telling my new friends, would be good for me, like the right kind of medicine, like a cold wind that would clean out my insides. So I think I've decided to tell them, open my mouth, wondering how to start at the beginning, which beginning I should choose, but instead find myself explaining that I've come to start a union, that their working conditions and pay are abhorrent, anyone can see that things here aren't right, and if we can organize, if we can all band together, if we can link arms and then hold our ground, I am sure there's a way for both pay and working conditions to improve. I'm talking and talking and don't know how to stop, not even sure where this idea came from, or how it replaced my desire to explain what happened before I arrived. But I've never been so interested in the past, always much more concerned with the future, and as I talk I find myself wondering if once again I have some feeling that the future exists, if I've discovered a new obsession, a new goal, that might replace the overwhelming destruction of past defeats. If I might be coming back to life.

I look around the circle at my new friends. They're not giving anything away, I can't tell if or how they're responding, if I'm in any way convincing, if they think I'm crazy or instead they're intrigued. We are speaking more quietly now, since so many of those in the field that surrounds us have gone or are going to sleep for the night. I look around, and for the first time I notice just how many tents have been set up, tents that are barely tents, pieces of cheap fabric held in place with a couple of sticks. So many of those here have nowhere else to go. I'm a bit drunk, or more, and so have no difficulty throwing my impasse into the circle—time to be direct, asking everyone, if they're still listening, what they think. A union is hard work to build and easy to break, one of them says, mainly sounding sad, most of us here don't have papers, if we fight they can round us up in a second, send us straight home. I'm listening, wanting to temper my response, but I can't, I'm too excited. They can't round up all of us, I find myself saying, almost thinking aloud, they need workers. They can't just let the fruit rot on the vine. Even if we manage to stop work for one day, or half a day, they would lose so much cash. It would be a reality. They would have to deal with us. Plus, they're not expecting it. We have the element of surprise. I have no idea if what I'm saying is true, if it makes any sense, and for a moment I worry that it's too much like before. I made a bad plan and followed it through until the end, had the piano wire in my pocket while the entire time it made no sense, hurtling towards such dismal results. But then I cheer myself up, thinking that before I had acted alone, had no help, and now I have my new friends, we can discuss, figure things out together, try to find some way.

1.

I am thinking about scapegoats, wondering if I'm in the process of becoming one. Back when I felt more firmly in charge, there were games I could play, moving the blame around. Now I hesitate, worrying it is too risky, could too easily backfire. Piano-idiot did this to me, making me second-guess myself at every turn, no longer pushing forward with impunity as I once did and have always done. It was only a simple physical attack, I don't understand how it undermined me so deeply, if that is in fact what is happening, or if it's instead something else I don't yet understand. Today there was a memo sent out to only a handful of top-level employees. I don't know if I was meant to be included in this memo, or if my inclusion was simply accidental, but I read it on the plane to Switzerland and, when I finally got to the hotel at midnight, lay awake thinking about what it said, lay awake practically all night instead of getting the sleep I would desperately need to get me through a series of carefully navigated meetings and lunches that had been scheduled for some time. The meetings would be difficult for many reasons, my exhaustion wouldn't help matters, and having the memo on my mind would make everything even worse.

It was basically a memo that had nothing to do with me, concerning certain protocols for what to do when things go wrong, more specifically for when things go wrong in one division and a completely different division experiences the most drastic, negative results, often in another part of the world. In the memo a single example is given: A manager allows a strike to escalate in a factory in China. This slows down production, and the roll-out date for a new product in France must be delayed. The product has already been announced, and bad publicity occurs, as well as understandably frustrated consumers. The product therefore does not meet its preliminary sales targets. The head of the division in France feels he is not to blame, he did everything right. He would like the blame to be placed where it is rightfully deserved, and the manager in China be forced to take responsibility for the delay. This memo suggests another solution, a solution that is overwhelmingly familiar to me, that a third party take the blame, someone who has little to do with the situation and who is clearly expendable. This is nothing if not the scapegoat department that I spent a certain period of my life developing, before finally deciding it was more trouble than it was worth.

The memo went on to explain that if either the manager in China or the manager in France were to be blamed, it would create unnecessary tensions between the divisions, divisions that will need to continue to work together, and work together quite closely, well into the undefined future. Any tensions starting now would most likely escalate, creating unforeseen problems, while reprimanding, or even firing, someone unimportant would create considerably less long-term collateral damage. And yet I couldn't read the memo without wondering, all night in this case, whether its logic might some day be applied to me, whether some day I would be the unimportant individual who gets the axe, and more specifically, if there were to be some future, large-scale crisis within the organization, whether firing me might be the most efficiently symbolic solution. As a notable, one could even say popular, figurehead, firing me would be a clear sign to the public that serious changes were being made within the organization, while at the same time leaving those actually responsible in the clear.

But why the fuck do I even care? Let them fire me. They were not my equals. I could eat a dozen of them for breakfast, and still, even at my age, whip up the energy to found another organization, from scratch, at least twice this size, all before noon. Or at least that is how I would have felt only a few years ago, and I still believe it, to a certain extent, still to this day. But I was also lying to myself if I didn't admit that something had changed. That first meeting in Zurich, already strained from my night of self-lacerating insomnia, began with a fight. My opponent claimed he had received little support from the head office, and used as his first example the fact that they sent me for this meeting, instead of sending someone more important. I don't know why he chose to begin the meeting with this slap to my face, and I was about to tear into him, annihilate him, leaving behind nothing but ashes, when, for some reason, even though it is rarely my style, I decided to attempt a few rounds of diplomacy to get the ball rolling. He was young—the youngest CEO the division ever had—and I wondered if he suffered from generational anxieties, fears that he wasn't at the same level as the founders, as my generation, and therefore needed to prove himself by knocking me down a few rungs. Or if his tactic was simply a sign of inexperience. Or maybe he only thought I was no longer particularly important and therefore he could take me.

So, if we can call it my attempt at diplomacy, I began by pointing out that it was not the role of the organization to serve each of the divisions; it was in fact the responsibility of each division to serve the organization, and if he felt he was not receiving enough 'attention,' perhaps it was because his division was underperforming, while at the top they had more important matters to attend to. If he wanted more attention, at the very least, he could begin by generating more profit. This did not go over well. Moreover, it irked me to refer to those 'at the top,' since in the past I had always been the top, there had never been anyone above me. He came back at me hard, claiming he had outperformed, generated more profit, than any other division in his hemisphere, and perhaps it was only because of his relative youth that he was not being taken seriously. Then I knew I had him. I started to relax, time for the real diplomacy to begin, gently explaining that by the time I was his age I wasn't just running one division, I was already running the entire organization, over one hundred and twenty divisions at that time, and if he felt people were discriminating against him because of his youth, I had an equal if not greater grievance, in that I felt some individuals, himself included, did not take me seriously because of my age, when in fact they should be making use of my considerable experience, unparalleled anywhere in the current business world, and, instead of attacking me at first sight, if he had one ounce of sense in his thick skull, he would be taking this opportunity to learn from me, since at this moment I was his best chance for advancement and—with that ridiculous chip on his shoulder, not to mention his general lack of social grace—he was flushing this one chance straight down the toilet.

He thought about it for a moment, then apologized. He was sure we could work together, for the good of his division and for the good of the organization. But then he corrected me. When I was his age I was not yet CEO of everything, that came ten years later. He still had ten years to beat my record and I shouldn't underestimate him. The Swiss were neutral, he explained, but that certainly didn't mean, silently, behind the scenes, they wouldn't kill when necessary.

2.

Initial plans to unionize slowly began to seem feasible. Word was spreading that this was the reason I had come, and though I often felt like an imposter, most of the workers instead treated me like an expert. Here, unlike in the past, I was someone who knew what needed to be done and how. Only, in reality, I wasn't that person at all. Or even that kind of person. Nonetheless, as I was learning, when you pretend to be something, you also gradually become it.

I was asleep in my cheap hotel room. Every night, as I lay down, I thought that perhaps tomorrow I should give up this room and go sleep in the field with the others, that this move would increase solidarity, but each morning for some reason I hesitated, still wanting a margin of difference between myself and the other workers. I was asleep when the door opened and a number of men quietly entered the room. They turned on the light, dragged me out of bed, threw me to the floor, and immediately started kicking me, one after the other, and I screamed, and they each kicked me again, and I screamed again and again until they momentarily stopped. "We could kill you right now and no one would care or notice," one of them said. I could barely look up, barely tell them apart, there were at least ten, "but we won't kill you now. We want the others to see what we've done, see what each of them will look like if they continue along with your idiotic scheme. You are an idiot, a moron, a piece of shit, and you must understand that if you continue, we will kill you." Then the kicking resumed, I don't know for how long, or for how long before I passed out, or how long until I came to again, but when I did they were gone.

I tended my wounds the best I could, then tried to sleep for a few hours, and I suppose I managed, dreamt of more men kicking me, as if the kicking would never stop, but at least I slept. In the morning, first thing, I checked out of the hotel. The clerk was unfazed by my two black eyes; he must have given them the key to my room but I didn't hold it against him. He most likely felt he had no choice. I bought a cheap tent in town, the same tent that so many of the others had already bought, and went to live in the field. I was in agony but decided to remain stoic, hoping that my example would serve to strengthen the general resolve.

It didn't take long for word to spread. In a few hours everyone knew what had happened to me, and I spent all day roaming the field, patiently explaining that they couldn't scare me and we wouldn't give up. There were so many different languages in that field, and it was often difficult to communicate. I was constantly searching for someone who could translate, even if it was only a few words. Together we would all pick a day, it had to be soon so we didn't lose momentum, and for just that one day work would completely stop. Just to show that it is possible, that we were capable and organized. They could beat me but they couldn't beat us all. This wasn't like some factory they could move overseas. The crops were growing here, and it was here they needed to be harvested. I insisted we keep our demands simple and direct. That they double all wages. If before you would get one dollar per token, soon you would get two. And that they cancel all deductions. They brought us here because they need us. They give us water and food because they need us hydrated and fed, ready to work. There was no reason for such things to be deducted from our basic wages. I spent years of my life reading shareholder reports, the years leading up to the bonfire, knew they could afford it, that it would barely make a dent in their bottom line. We might not get everything we wanted, but we'd get something, the situation would definitely improve. However, I also knew the flaw in my plan, that we were dealing only with subcontractors, it was unlikely our demands would reach the people who mattered, the people who actually had the power to grant them. This was an obstacle I did not yet know how to surmount.

That night there was an enormous meeting. I began by quickly, and I believe efficiently, outlining my proposal for a one-day strike. Then I moved on to the main obstacle: that because our bosses here were only subcontractors, the important people—their clients, the people who paid them and therefore had the actual power to meet our demands—would not be affected, would most likely never hear about our strike. Rapidly the meeting got rolling, everyone throwing out ideas, jokes and suggestions in every possible language, while others tried to translate, and yet, miraculously, I did not yet know why, people were for the most part speaking one at a time, interrupting each other, but letting everyone have a turn. This left me slightly in shock, even now when I think about it. An objection was made that judging what had already been done to me, if we proceeded some of us would most certainly be killed. And several others, each in their own language, countered that the way we were living here, the way we were treated, we might as well be dead already, that things couldn't get worse. Things can always get worse, someone yelled from the back, when you reach hell there is always another hell underneath. Yet he said it in a way that made us all laugh; he sort of honked his voice on the word hell, making it sound less like a place, or state of mind, and more like a vaudeville routine.

I tried to move the debate away from the question of whether we should strike, and towards the main obstacle: how to let the corporations, the buyers, know we are striking, so there is at least some chance they would meet our demands. Soon everyone was shouting out ideas:

"We can all get on buses, show up at their front door."

"Where are we going to get fucking buses?"

"We can hijack the buses, the buses they use to take us to work."

"If we steal just one bus, the cops will chase us down in a second. We'll all end up dead or deported."

"Where are the head offices?"

People yelled out the names of cities, seemingly at random, also the names of companies, names they had seen on the sides of eighteen-wheelers, or on cardboard boxes, as, on rare occasions, they had to pack the produce themselves. And I recognized the name of every division. It was like a revelation, like something religious. Had I or had I not already known that the main client for most of the farms that surrounded us were divisions of my former employer? I must have read it, seen the names, many times over, back when I was compiling my reports. But it was only at this precise moment that I fully made the connection. Of course they were the ones profiting from this exploitation. They were always the ones.

1.

I'm losing my nerve, or perhaps the bulk of it is already gone. At the same time, from the outside, few cracks show, no one can tell. No one can tell and yet everyone knows. It's now as if there were three strikes against me. The first strike was the takeover bid. We successfully defeated them, kept our organization intact, but in the ensuing scuffle lost Emmett, and in some sense our legal difficulties have remained constant, at times overwhelming, since that uneasy victory. The second strike was the crash. We came out okay, but it is possible to speculate that a younger, more effective version of myself would have come out considerably ahead, as did so many others. The third strike was the murder attempt. No one knows exactly what happened, or why, and therefore malicious rumours run rampant. And then the thing I so rarely even consider, which is in fact the forth strike, that I am getting old, and there are many young men out there hoping to some day have my job. The killer knows what it's like to be a killer, yet can barely imagine what things feel like on the other side of the equation.

The more I worry about it, the more it occurs to me that the book, both books—the one I wrote and the one written, on the verge of their hack-divorce, only to slander me—also had something of a negative effect. Here I am once again on an airplane, travelling somewhere with the stated aim of gaining an overview. Yet as I travel I'm learning little new information about the overall state of the organization, and a great deal about my own mental state, which I am forced to admit is poor. I want to blame piano-idiot, but it is never wise to blame others. I have always been a man who believes that every problem has a solution; it is only a matter of strategy, will and luck. The woman in the seat beside me is reading and I decide that I should read as well. In the seat pocket in front of me I have already placed five slim volumes of poetry, the finalists for this year's prize.

Shuffling through the books I suddenly realize that one of them is by him, that bastard Marxist who tore up our cheque in front of everyone. He spits in our face and we have the good graces to nominate him again. Suddenly I'm seized by an anger that wants to explode, like a bomb in this plane, tearing it in two and dropping it out of the sky. He spits in our face and yet we're so generous, so benevolent, we care so much about poetry that we reward him by nominating him a second time. If he was here in front of me now, I would tear out his throat. The woman beside me thinks I'm having a heart attack, asks me if I'm okay, and, I don't know why, I have to vent, I end up telling her the entire story. It turns out she is also a poet, or at least she was when she was younger, before she got married. She put out two volumes, asks if I've heard of them and I lie, saying that I had. She then has the nerve to go on to tell me that the idiot Marxist is one of her favourite poets, that his talent clearly transcends his politics, and our committee did the right thing in nominating him a second time.

Now I want to tear out her throat as well, but at the same time I'm beginning to catch hold of myself, to calm down. He is only a poet, and I am a billionaire, and I know at the end of the day there is no real way he can hurt me. He has no public voice, only a few readers, while I have every newspaper in the free world. That's why we chose to sponsor a prize for poets and not a prize for movie actors, who wouldn't need the extra money anyways, but would always be happy to receive any extra attention. The middle-aged poet beside me is clearly worried that I'm still upset. I can tell she thinks I'm far more infuriated than the situation warrants, and she is most likely right, but I hate feeling weak. I know there is another way of viewing the situation, that by nominating him a second time we are in fact showing our strength, showing we are impervious to his attacks, that they do not affect us, but I am too angry, cannot bring myself to see it from this angle.

Wanting to change the subject, I ask the woman what her husband does, and find out that he works for us, which is not as much of a coincidence as it first seems, the organization always uses this airline, which we own. And then I realize she will get home and tell her husband, tell him that on the plane she met the big CEO of everything and that, of all things, I was fuming about a book of poetry. It's almost too ridiculous to believe, but the story will come from his wife so he'll believe it, and will most likely tell anyone willing to listen. Now, on top of feeling furious, I also feel humiliated, and I'm stuck on this plane with nowhere to go and nothing to do. I ask a few more questions about her husband, learning he's actually quite high up on the energy side of things, which is probably why she is sitting here beside me in first class. If he tells everyone he knows, it means that many of the employees I deal with on a daily basis will also hear this story, the story of the big boss getting all worked up over a poetry book. For a moment I consider asking her to tell no one, to keep what I've told her only between her and me, but I know enough about human nature to know it would be futile. I am a stranger, she owes me nothing, and a good story, especially one that humiliates the powerful, is a story that must be told.

2.

I put off making the call for almost a week. I don't know how to begin or exactly what my strategy should be. I have a plan but at the same time realize it's no plan at all. I survey my argument again and again: before you had a plan, which I fucked, but your plan was little more than a desire for revenge. What I am proposing is justice. Justice is better than revenge. I suspect that Emmett cares nothing for justice, that he is deeply and utterly immoral. But I'm counting on the fact that he still wants to attack, and that he will see the benefit of attacking from the moral high ground, see it is more sustainable, a long-term game. When the poor organize, unionize, demand their fair share, the rich make less, over time gradually becoming less powerful. They are still rich, but no longer so omnipotent. Someone can take them on, and if you win just one battle, others will be tempted to try as well. Emmett was never a true friend, but he knows me. There might still be some tattered remnants of trust.

But procrastination takes on a life of its own, and there were at least two more meetings with everyone before I finally found the energy to make the call. There was a kind of fear at these meetings. We had no legal right to strike, not even for one day, and our illegal action would certainly be met with violence. We had no idea how much or what form it would take, but most likely it would appear soon, before the strike, in order to prevent it, scare us straight. At each meeting, I saw it as my job to counterbalance the fear with something else: hope, reason, confidence—anything, I didn't really know what would work best or what would help. Fear was also a reasonable reaction to what we were about to attempt, and I didn't exactly know what courage was or where it might come from. Did I have courage when I wrapped the piano wire around that bastard's neck? Was courage what blinded me to the fact that my plan was too narrow, was unlikely to work? My fear wasn't of violence, for in a way I felt I was already dead. My fear was that I was leading these people towards a catastrophe just as foolish as the one I had barely survived before coming here, and that they would blame me for it, that they would end up hating me as much as I sometimes—especially in the first days I arrived— had hated myself.

And yet these meetings filled me with such a sense of possibility. All the different languages shouting out suggestions and doubts in every direction, as others rushed to translate, to keep up. It wasn't that any of us knew what we were doing, though I suppose many assumed that I at least partially did. It was a feeling. A feeling and an energy. That we were about to attempt something that just a few weeks ago no one here had even imagined possible. A few weeks before, I had gone to the library and copied the following onto a scrap of paper:

> A useful starting point for differentiating types of workers' bargaining power is Erik Olin Wright's distinction between associational and structural power. Associational power consists of "the various forms of power that result from the formation of collective organizations of workers" (most importantly, trade unions and political parties). Structural power, in contrast, consists of the power that accrues to workers "simply from their location . . . in the economic system." Wright further divides "structural" power into two subtypes. The first subtype of structural power (which we shall call marketplace bargaining power) is the power that "results directly from tight labour markets." The second subtype (which we shall call workplace bargaining power) is the power that results "from the strategic location of a particular group of workers within a key industrial sector."

> Marketplace bargaining power can take several forms including (1) the possession of scarce skills that are in demand by employers, (2) low levels of general unemployment and (3) the ability of workers to pull out of the labour market entirely and survive on non-wage sources of income. Workplace bargaining power, on the other hand, accrues to workers who are enmeshed in tightly integrated production processes, where a localized work stoppage in a key node can cause disruptions on a much wider scale than the stoppage itself. Such bargaining power had been in evidence when

entire assembly lines have been shut down by a stoppage in one segment of the line, and when entire corporations relying on the just-in-time delivery of parts have been brought to a standstill by railway workers' strikes.

What kind of bargaining power did we really have and what were the consequences of trying to make use of it? The produce was being grown here and now. If it wasn't harvested it would simply rot on the vine. It couldn't just be picked up and moved somewhere else, and everyday it was left there to rot money was being lost. How much money could they afford to lose before it would begin to hurt? In one sense the answer was a virtually infinite amount. There were so many different divisions of the organization. One division could bleed money for years while others picked up the slack. But I knew it also didn't quite work that way. Every division needed to pull its weight, and in divisions that posted considerable losses, those at the top were chastised, could easily lose their jobs. Or the whole division could be sold off, chopped up for spare parts. So there were clearly many in each division whose lives depended on keeping the profits flowing.

Then there was the maze of subcontractors in which we found ourselves enmeshed. Each subcontractor might sell produce to many different corporations. It was the subcontractors who would feel the pain first, who would immediately lose money if the harvest were to pause, who would be fired first, easily replaced by another subcontractor long before any division, much less the larger organization, felt a fucking thing. But I didn't want to go after the subcontractors, they were relatively powerless to help us. They drove their buses on and off the field. They packed off the crates and, much like us, received a small sum for each one, keeping most of the profits, kicking only a bit of dust in our direction. If the organization pays the subcontractors more, we won't see even a glimpse of it. What we need is for the organization to demand that each of its subcontractors pay more, double the price for each token, that they insist and are willing to cough up for it, to pay more on the condition that our lot improves. For this to happen we must embarrass them. The price, relative to their overall profits, is small, at the very least a small cost in order to save face, to increase the possible illusion they are humane corporate citizens. How to get their attention and make sure they know why? It feels impossible but also too late to turn back. I have the strange anxiety that men with guns will march onto the field one night and simply kill us all, every last one.

1.

I think I saw Emmett. He was far away so I couldn't be sure. But as I stared at the figure in the distance, trying to decide if it was actually him and, if so, if he had spotted me in return, I started to see the entire matter in a different light. The man who used to be my closest friend in the world had, in all likelihood, attempted to have me killed. What's more he had done so incompetently. What does this fact, if it is a fact, tell me about my life, about friendship, about loyalty? You can tell so much about a man's character by his friends and how he treats them. Who exactly are my friends now? I think I saw Emmett in the distance yet didn't know if I should chase him down or let him go. I try to recall our last actual conversation but cannot. For the last three or four months, before he cut off all ties, we were both up to our necks in lawyers. And Emmett is a lawyer, I am definitely not. I believe when he realized it would most likely be him taking the fall, that I was selling him down the river, he became more of a lawyer than ever. He's now tried to have me killed once. Why aren't I more paranoid? Why aren't I more on guard, nervous that he will attempt to have me killed again? Do I think I'm invincible? But nothing adds up. Emmett was never the type to mess around. If he wanted me dead I would have been dead long ago. Or something went wrong. I'm nervous I'm becoming less effective and, over the same period, perhaps Emmett has become less effective as well.

The day I thought I saw him in the distance was a strange one. I was without my driver, walking through the streets. I suspect I wanted to be alone that day. So often there are people swarming around me: picking me up at the airport, driving me places, ushering me into meetings. What I notice is when you start to be haunted by feelings of failure your desire to be alone increases. I was only home for a day before my next trip. Tomorrow I would, once again, be ushered around by strangers and, before I was swept back up into my ongoing survey of the world, I wanted at least a few hours to reflect. I still believe, if you were a camera in the corner of the room, watching me, following me through the streets, everything would appear to be in order. The cracks in the façade were not yet showing; the oncoming rush of possible difficulties remained imperceptible, too subtle to be noticed or suspected by anyone but me. It still seemed so possible that my life would continue like this without anything ever quite going completely wrong. I would travel for a few years, get the fullest possible overview of our organization, then return home to run it, shore up my remaining power, perhaps end up even more in charge than I had been in the past. This was possible, even likely. But unfortunately it was not the only possibility.

I was wandering alone, without a driver or a bodyguard, and perhaps seeing Emmett in the distance had made me nervous. I wondered if Emmett could still harm me and, as I did so, also had a slight pang of friendship-residue, wondering if he was all right, how he was doing. Since there were no handlers shuttling me around, since I had managed to escape for a few hours, I thought it might be a good moment to visit a prostitute. At my age I was beginning to consider that prostitutes were the best solution. A trophy wife, a woman young enough for me to completely desire her, seemed in bad taste, though so many other CEOs of my generation apparently had no problem with it. And maybe I would try that again some day, but not today. Today a prostitute seemed like the best option, a reminder that a pure economic transaction was the most clean, the most precise, method for fulfilling desires and needs.

I know business, I know money, and therefore I know that they are always slightly troubled by the realities of sexual prostitution, since sex is something that can never be stripped clean. Economics, like money itself, wants to keep pushing everything towards abstraction. The more we're able to think of things as being only things, the more malleable they become, the more we can manipulate and play them. It might be true that sex and desire are also abstract—the person I am fucking is never only that person but always, also, my fantasy of them—but it seems that fucking will always be fucking. There is always some physical aspect to it that doesn't want to be reduced. You can't help but sense your body right there on the line. One million apples or one million typewriters easily land on a spreadsheet, but one million fucks feel out of place.

Does this have something to do with freedom? With consumer options? I cannot go out and get one million apples for free.

But right now, all over the world, one million fucks are actually taking place without anyone paying a cent. And though you can always find a few men, perhaps also a few women, who would prefer to pay for it (I, today, might be one of these men), for most of those million they would absolutely prefer not to think of their fucking as a transaction. This doesn't mean they particularly mind thinking of some aspect of it as exchange, the man paying for dinner being the most obvious and clichéd example, but that slight buffer of dinner between fucking and economics appears to be a relative necessity for most.

2.

During that time I would frequently go to the library. It was an escape from the field, a place to think about what we were doing, envision strategy, read books that question our current approach and give pertinent examples from history. So many things had been tried before, succeeded or failed, or succeeded for a while only to fail much later and more painfully. Then there was the day I realized there was a piano in the library, an upright, pushed into a corner, covered with a black sheet. For several weeks I only noticed the piano, but then one day I went to the desk and asked about it, asked if it was in tune. They believed it was, someone came to tune it several times each year. And I don't know why—I was so sure I had left all of that completely behind and never wanted to look back—but I asked if I could play it when the library was empty, which seemed to be most of the time. They said I could, it would be nice to have music at times. So on certain days, after an hour or two spent reading, I would walk over to the piano, neatly fold up the black cloth, sit down, and trying not to think too much about what it meant or why, play for a while. It seemed to be the only thing that would calm me, where for a moment I might forget the violence, the constant and immanent threat.

I don't know when exactly I realized I was no longer playing Mozart or Bach, that I was now playing something else, almost remembered songs I must have first heard in childhood. But these melodies I found myself playing, sketching them out as I went, half-remembered and likely incorrect—from a time before we lost everything and a time before I knew that life was going to be so hard—gave me a sort of difficult-to-pin-down confidence. They suggested another world, a world that existed before all this shit we currently found ourselves in, a world that might still be purring gracefully along long after all of this has completely burned to the ground. That there is not only one time, but different times. There is the time of the field, rushing to get on the buses so you can harvest a few meagre dollars of produce to be shipped to neon-lit supermarkets, where those who purchase it will not think for a moment of the labour that brought each item into their thoughtlessly greedy hands. And then there is the time of these scant melodies, which were here long before any of us were born and will likely continue to transform, continue to be sung and hummed and whistled long after all of us, all of this, is gone. This other time didn't care if we lived or died, doesn't care if it's me remembering each note and stringing them together, or someone else in some other way, sense or age. If something disappears there is always the possibility it might return. These songs have existed in different forms, made slow or fast, with different words or slight variations on the same words, and if they've existed for so long there is no reason they wouldn't continue to exist. I didn't even know which folk songs they were. Or when I first or last heard them. Or if I would ever hear them sung properly again. All of these thoughts and emotions ran through me with greater and greater force as I sat at the piano and quietly played.

One afternoon I was playing, lost in the music. I worried each time I played that I became lost in the music a little bit more, that maybe someday I wouldn't want to come back, that this refuge from the tension and potential violence I would soon have to return to—a violence I'd done everything to incite—would once again become a refuge I wanted to make my permanent home. Why leave something comforting to return to the nerve-wrecking slam of the world? On this particular afternoon I was so lost I don't know how long it had been before I noticed someone listening and watching me. She wasn't threatening in any way, just an older woman in a library who saw there was music and decided to take it in. But when I turned to face her I had a thought, or feeling, I don't think I ever had before. I looked at her, she smiled, and my first impression was that maybe she was about the same age my mother would have been if my mother was still alive. This startled me. Coming here, being surrounded with people who looked more like me, speaking a language from my childhood, playing these melodies from another lifetime and another world—clearly all of this had unlocked something that was now taking on a life of its own, out of my control. I looked at her and started to cry. I was staring straight at her, my face streaming with tears, but she met my eyes calmly, completely unfazed. I think she said something like: you play beautifully. I hope I said thank you as I continued to cry and, since I was now crying too hard to speak, turned back to the piano, sliding back into the old songs. I hoped she would be gone by the time I finished, I played and played for such a long time, yet when I was done she was still there. She again said that I played beautifully and asked if she could take me to lunch.

Over lunch I learned she'd heard I was trying to start a union. In fact everyone knew. It was the most gossip-worthy thing that had happened here in a very long time. She had come to the library to find me, and didn't have words to describe how unexpected it was to walk in and see me at the piano, hunched over it like I'd been caught doing something illicit. She came to find me because her husband had been a union leader. He died over twenty years ago. She said that he died, she was used to presenting it that way now, but what she meant was that he had been killed. She worried I might be killed as well, in a way she wanted to warn me, but then thought that was stupid, since I likely already knew what a dangerous mess I was in.

She also wanted to talk strategy, wanted to help if she could. Because of her husband she knew a great deal about these things. As we talked and I answered her many questions, as I tried to explain how I saw the situation and what we eventually hoped to do, I could see a kind of pain dawning on her face. I didn't have to ask why. I could see she was shocked by how little I knew, how little experience I had, the overwhelming degree to which I was in over my head. I tried to imagine what she was thinking: that her husband had been so much more skilled and experienced in these matters and even he was killed. At the same time I saw something else, that the more she understood the more she wanted to help, the more she understood just how much she could. If I knew so little then she definitely knew more.

I started to think of her as 'the mentor.' She would come to the library, listen to me play. I would show her the books I'd been reading and she would always have something to say. Her thinking was so precise and clean. She had been through all of this before, packing so many possibilities into just a few thoughts. When I was clearly wrong, she cut me down with a joke and we'd laugh about it together. It felt like the first time I had really laughed in many lifetimes. I was talking to so many people, each day in the fields, quietly joking and laughing with man after man, their ideas, their fears. So many fears and I took them all in. I start to think fear is the most furious part of courage. Knowing how full and real and justified your fears are but still not letting them stop you. Each day I would wake up and tell myself: if I die here in the fields, shot by police or beaten by whatever henchmen the subcontractors can pay a few dollars to do so, I have to believe all of this will have been worth it, was the right thing to do. If we don't make a union now, perhaps we'll still form the groundwork for some future actors to learn from our mistakes, make it a reality in some distant future. Like the folk songs I didn't know I still knew, but came through me when I sat down at the piano, when I was least expecting them. This idea that even in the fields, with nothing but sweat, we could raise our lot by working together was an idea that now existed, and would keep coming back again and again until it finally had its day.

1.
I had left the money on the dresser, much as I had so many times before. Four thousand in cash. I had come, come hard, and it winded me, an orgasm like a punch in the gut, reminding me of my age—a thought I was finding increasingly unpleasant as I travelled the world, worried I was devolving into

a mere figurehead. I was resting for a moment, gathering the energy so we could go again (I always prefer it more than once) and as I rested we were talking. She was a new one. There were four or five I usually had to choose from, but this afternoon this one was new. Then she told me she had read my book, and I must have gone pale, because she asked me if I was all right, if I wanted a glass of water. "Which book," I asked. She told me she had read the one I wrote, the one with my picture on the cover. I was about to ask her what she thought then thought better of it, felt I didn't actually want to hear her answer, worried she was about to tell me something extremely unpleasant about myself, but then asked her what she thought about it. "It was brave of you to write," she said, considering her words closely, perhaps also worried she was about to tell me something I didn't exactly want to hear. "You told things about yourself that a lot of men wouldn't tell."

"Like what?"

"Like your friendship. How you behaved when Emmett ended up on the other side."

"How did I behave?"

"You felt betrayed. But you were also honest about it. Admitted you were complicit in the problem. I've had a few friendships go sour. I know how painful these things can be."

"You think I was honest?"

"Someone else might have blamed it all on the other guy. You took responsibility. That shows character, takes guts."

I wondered if I was just paying for sex or also paying for thera-py. Or for praise, for an attractive young woman to praise me with or without reason. She continued:

"I meet a lot of rich men. They always blame the other guy and I never believe them. Most often, whatever you accuse someone else of is probably the exact thing you do the most. Strange that's how our minds work: denying our own shit and magically inserting it into the other one's intentions. But you didn't do that. You owned up."

I was searching my memory, desperately trying to remember what I had actually said about Emmett and his departure. What had she read, and had I actually written it or did she find it between the lines? Was this yet another reason people were now suspicious of me, because I had admitted in writ-ing to the betrayal of one of my closest friends? I wonder how many of those I dealt with on a daily basis had actually read my book? Or worse, heard rumours about its contents, ru-mours that exaggerated certain aspects of my misdeeds.

"You're telling me all this very calmly. Do you do always talk this way to your clients?"

"You're new. But I don't actually see so many new ones. Most of the men come back, at least the ones I like. They're rich, they can go fuck any girl in the world, but they choose to come here. And I think it's because I'm honest with them. I mean, I'm not tactless. But I talk to them, tell it like it is."

"What you said could have made me angry. Weren't you afraid I'd get angry?"

"Why would you get angry?"

"It's a backhanded compliment."

"I don't do backhanded compliments. What I say, I mean."

"What would you have done if I'd gotten angry?"

"There's a number to call. Five minutes to get here and then the bodyguards throw you out. But five minutes is still long enough for a man to kill a woman. I've called it a few times and I've never had a problem. Are you angry?"

I was getting angry but didn't want to admit it. I believed her for some reason, believed she was being honest with me, and it made me wonder how many people lied to my face day after day. We fuck two more times and then I was out on the street with nowhere particular to go. Maybe I should go into therapy. I've always thought therapy was bullshit, for the other ones, the ones who couldn't handle it, but perhaps I was in the process of joining their ranks. I decided to walk home. As a young man I used to walk everywhere, and I found myself wondering how much I missed in only seeing the world through a limousine window. So I walked. And as I walked, my mind cleared by sex, I tried to examine my predicament from every possible angle. There were so many angles, so many ways of seeing the matter, but the more I walked the more it seemed to me that in fact there was only one. Piano-idiot did this to me. He killed some aspect of my confidence, made it blindingly clear that I was not omnipotent, could die at any moment. That money would not save me. Whether or not Emmett had hired him started to seem irrelevant. Emmett had a reason to hate me.

Piano-idiot came on like an unexpected storm. There was of course a way that money could save me: more bodyguards, more surveillance, or simply the resources to make myself scarce. But if money could save me from certain dangers, it couldn't save me from paranoia. I didn't want to hide. Should I find piano-idiot or should I simply forget him? Should I find Emmett? What to do with this sudden revelation, that everyone has to face sooner or later, that there are more years in my past than there are in my future? What do I honestly want to do with the years I have left? Do I just want to nail down my legacy or do I still have a few good tricks?

I realized I had walked all the way home. The concierge buzzed me in. I took a long hot shower, and carefully thought over whether or not I had anything to do before I left again early tomorrow. The dry cleaning had been delivered and was already packed. I had already been checked in. All of this was done for me without even having to ask. If I think back to what it was like when I was starting out, this is a level of effortless comfort I would have barely dreamed of. I knew I wanted the world, but in a way thought I would need to keep working hard for it right until the end. I still work hard, but so many things are now taken care of. I didn't lose my temper with that prostitute. I really wonder if I'm going soft. A soft life makes soft thoughts, soft actions. But when you're getting older, its also difficult, even pathetic, to pretend that you're not.

I had been travelling for so many months, a world tour or never-ending vacation. The organization was so large it at times seemed endless. My apartment had been cleaned today, while I was out, and it was pristine, spotless. It would be cleaned again, I believe several times, before I returned. It looked like an apartment in which no one ever lived. I look at the bookshelf, row after row of poetry. I was hoping to find a copy of my own book but then remember I got rid of it. There was a moment not so long ago when I was standing in front of this shelf and acted on the strong urge to get every single copy out of my space, out of every single one of my houses. I believe I did a thorough job. It was something about the way my own face stared out at me from the cover. If I think about this now, it seems like the action of someone slowly losing his grip. I wonder why I'm so tired, then realize I probably walked more today than I have in many years. I set my alarm before going to sleep. As usual, the driver will pick me up three hours before my flight. I'll eat breakfast in the first-class lounge. I go to the shelf and pick out a few poetry books to take with me. A few old favourites and a few I haven't gotten to yet. As I slip the books into my carry-on, it occurs to me that there really are a lot of poems about death, that I've always read many poems about dying, but had almost never noticed them before. They were always the ones I lightly skimmed, and I thought that maybe I could start reading these poems more carefully. It was almost nothing, but it was also a decision about my life.

2.

I bring the mentor with me to the next meeting. Nighttime. A few hundred of us huddled around a large brushwood fire. I let the mentor begin: "What we're here to discuss, to work towards, is not simply a one-day strike or a longer strike. It's something else, the idea of solidarity, of standing up for yourself but doing so all together." A few of the workers who felt fluent enough to translate were doing so, as small groups of other workers gathered around them. The mentor paced herself accordingly, making a statement then leaving room for translation. The effect was poignant, as the murmuring of different languages filled each pause.

"Solidarity doesn't mean we all need to agree on everything. It doesn't even mean we must come together on every point." Another pause for translation. "It simply means we pick a few topics around which to all push in the same direction. It might seem that being here, some of you without papers, waiting for the buses to come, you have no basic rights. But where there are profits there are possibilities, the possibility to get a fair share of the wealth each of you create." I looked around. I didn't know exactly how old the mentor was; she had that kind of timeless energy it was difficult to pin down, but she spoke with such experience and authority. Everyone was listening in a different way, with greater respect.

"These are all questions of principle on which it is fairly easy to agree. What is more difficult are questions of strategy, of tactics. We know the bosses possess an almost infinite greed, and will not give an inch unless we forcibly take it. The question of how we take it—this question of strategy—has a great deal to do with whether we succeed or fail. A one-day strike might seem like a good strategy at first glance, but let's consider the matter more fully." Another pause. I feel nervous about what she'll say next. "If we strike for one day it's like a warning shot. It does show we are organized, that we have the strength and power to bring everything to a halt. But it also shows our hand. It gives the bosses a chance to consider their next move, to retaliate. We might have only one bullet and we shouldn't waste it on a warning. Like David versus Goliath, we should take our best aim and, if possible, use this single bullet for the kill."

I didn't know she was going to say this. She should have consulted me first. This was a major shift in direction. But she knows so much more than me, is so much more experienced. I hope against hope that she is considering these matters with the full seriousness they deserve. As others finish translating, a new intensity comes over the gathering. She lets this intensity settle before continuing. "What I am proposing is that we strike with the intention to win. Which means we must keep the strike going until our demands are met." She looks over at me and I'm not quite sure how to interpret it. Is she looking for support, that I have her back despite the fact that she's so full of surprises. Or is her look more arrogant, as if to say: look, this is how it's done. "So what are these demands exactly? In my opinion, doubling the amount for each token is still thinking small, holds us in the realm of piecework. We must think bigger than that. A basic hourly wage in keeping with the national standard. You are the lowest paid workers in this country and that is not acceptable. In my opinion we should also be given protective gear to shield each of you from the harmful effects of pesticides. And the elimination of all deductions would be the final, clear choice. Three reasonable demands. Anyone who says they cannot be achieved suffers from a lack of imagination."

What happened next was something I'll never forget. At the time I couldn't quite follow it, so many questions, doubts and intensities through which I viewed the situation. Each person who spoke, with or without translation, doubled down on their commitment to this plan and their desire to win these demands at all costs. These three demands were repeated again and again, and each time they seemed more possible, more obvious, more like something we all must do. Something felt clear to me, the mentor was a voice we had been waiting for. I'm not sure I'd ever had a feeling quite like that, a feeling, almost overwhelming, that there was actually strength in numbers. That there were enough of us here in the dust to win. After everyone had their say (we must have spoken for several hours) I found myself walking along the outer edge of the field with the mentor. We were both supercharged, I could sense this energy coming from her and between us. But as we continued to walk in silence, she was also growing pensive, lost in thought, as if the intensity of her earlier speech was now draining away, leaving her with nothing. I was about to ask if she was all right when she started.

—That didn't go how I thought.

—How did you think it would go?

—I thought there would be more resistance. That they'd resist more.

I considered what she was saying. When I first stumbled upon the field, when I first proposed the idea of a union to avoid having to explain how I ended up here, I was expecting to be told it was impossible, a stupid idea, that I should go back where I came from and keep my stupid ideas to myself. But almost the opposite had happened. People here were ready for the gust of fresh air that our arrival represented, ready for a fight, to stand up for themselves. I wondered if it had anything to do with something I had felt since arriving, something I was never quite able to put into words. I now found myself wondering if this wordless feeling had to do with having nothing left to lose. A cliché that here in the fields felt worse than true.

—You wanted them to resist.

—I didn't want anyone to do anything. I wanted to test the waters. See what was possible. And right away I learned something that frightens me. The waters are favourable. Just about anything is possible.

—Why does that frighten you?

—I don't actually think we can win.

—Why not? What else do we need?

—I keep asking myself what my husband would do. But he's dead. And he never had to deal with anything like this. We used to strategize together. I always felt I knew just as much as he did. Perhaps that's why I came to find you. I wanted to put that feeling to the test. I wanted my chance.

—What would he have done?

—We need a war chest. We need resources. We need food and water, enough for the strike to last months, enough for as long as it lasts. Do you know anyone?

It was then I told her about Emmett. I didn't tell her everything. I sketched in the details as lightly as possible. I tried to stay focused on the fact that I was planning to call him, that he was someone who wanted to help (which might have been a lie, but I was hoping it was true). She was also brainstorming who she could call, friends and colleagues of her husband. People who might send food and water, but also who might come here, fight alongside us. She was listing names as we walked. Her husband had had many friends.

1.

Everyone is replaceable. If one million workers go on strike, we get rid of them and find one million more. Some of those workers might find new jobs, end up all right, while others might fall on hard times, have difficulty making ends meet, starve or even die. But we all die sooner or later. Of course, if they replace me, it releases the golden parachute and nothing in my material life suffers or changes. But apart from that slight difference it's the same. They can replace one million workers just as easily as they can replace me; no matter how talented, qualified or indispensable I think I might be, there's always someone else who can do the job.

These questions of downsizing seem to be filling my mind because, here on the flight, I've been reading about strikes. It seems we are living in a new golden age of strikes, a new wave of divisions and subdivisions that suddenly feel it's their God-given right to unionize. The report is awash with statistics: ten years ago there were seventy-two strikes, five years ago one hundred and twenty-eight, last year, which is the focus of the report, there were apparently two hundred and thirty-six. I sit on the plane reading all this, trying to understand what it means, wondering whether I should simply put the report down and return to one of the poetry books.

I stare at the report, at page after page of charts and statistics, and think to myself that it is a document about a zeitgeist. I know enough about labour history to know that workers strike when they have good enough reason to believe they can win something: more money or better conditions. What is it in the air that once again makes those bastards believe they can win? What I notice most is the degree to which these work stoppages appear to cover more and more distance over time. There is a map on page eighty-two of the report, each dot representing an instance of labour trouble that occurred over the past year, and the dots seem so evenly spread out across the surface of the globe. What we have traditionally done, moving production from one part of the world to another in order to avoid labour unrest, no longer feels as convenient.

Considering how many divisions actually fall within the auspices of the organization, two hundred and thirty-six strikes actually aren't that many. In the conclusion of the report, I learn that one hundred and fifty of them were put down without any union formation, and one hundred of those without making any salary or workplace concessions. So last year there were in fact only eighty-six successful strikes, a pittance, and yet still the zeitgeist so clearly seems to be saying: we believe we can win. Last year it was two hundred and thirty-six. In five years will it be five hundred, or in ten years a thousand? What if all the divisions and subdivisions manage to come together and strike at the same time? This seems impossible, but sitting here on this intercontinental flight, perhaps feeling more than a little paranoid, I have the strange feeling that nothing is impossible.

Then I turn the question around and come at it from another angle. The organization as a whole makes a certain margin of profit. If we give more to every single worker in every single division, this margin of profit would be reduced. But how much could it be reduced before the organization was no longer profitable? What's more, if on top of this you were to take a small percentage of the salaries of all upper management, such as myself, let's say three or four per cent, and redistribute it among the workers, to what extent would this gesture ameliorate their protests or concerns? Clearly there was almost infinite room to play, cat and mouse or any other game we felt up for. Every zeitgeist is perhaps also a game, and this game is being played on a field we could clearly call our own. I wondered if this might be my road back into the limelight: the great dealmaker, the negotiator, riding the crest of the zeitgeist towards a new era of labour-management relations. But it was also a dangerous game, showing my throat to more reactionary forces within the organization who want little more than the most possible work for the lowest dollar. If they have a chance to do me in, there is no question they will not hesitate for a moment.

I'm still thinking about what that Italian kid said about virtuosity, that his generation are virtuosos who will use their virtuosity to reorganize the means of production to their greatest benefit. If this can even be considered a legitimate threat, one possible recourse might be to simply make them an offer they can't refuse. I worry I'm becoming desperate, going soft, willing to consider any option that might fully reenergize my drifting reputation. I put down the report and pick up one of the poetry books. Flipping absentmindedly through the pages, I have this feeling I often have trying to read poetry: all these poets are the same. When dealing with something one apparently doesn't want to actually deal with, this is always the easiest way out: it's all the same. They all look the same, they all say the same things, they are a cliché of a self-parody of a cliché. All the poets searching for some clear, striking phrase or image that will more precisely reflect their position or some aspect of their lives. All the strikers demanding more money, more rights, more consumer goods, more dignity. I stare at the pages of poetry but feel distracted, unable to focus.

What are the clichés that accurately reflect me, that me and my class of assholes seem to say over and over again, like super-elite broken records. That the poor are lazy, that we work harder than everyone else and deserve every penny we make (in my particular case, this happens to be true), that we are the global class and therefore effortlessly, with great skill and determination, run the world. That finance is complicated; not everyone can effectively understand it, and it should be left in the hands of those of us who do. These clichés are almost poems. Depending on the situation, I myself have said similar things, but I've never completely believed them. Perhaps I've never completely believed anything, always searching for the angle that will help me overcome the next immediate obstacle, while at the same time trying to keep my sixth sense honed in on the long game. I've never been particularly sure that I've deserved anything. I like to gamble and I like to win. And, at the end of the day, there's actually no such thing as cheating. Now, halfway through this fucking losing streak, I can't seem to stop asking myself which dice to roll and where. I can't remain in crisis forever. Sooner or later I'll have to make my next move. Sooner or later I'll have to come up for air.

2.

I am staring at my cheaper-than-cheap cell phone. It was the cheapest one they had. I remember the salesman, three or four years ago, assuring me that I would only be happy with a better one. And I remember looking him in the eyes and smiling as I told him: no, I want the cheapest one. I have no money. Whatever is cheapest will be best for me. It still works perfectly. I hardly ever use it and it always works. I am staring at the phone because I know it's time to call him. I don't want to, almost sure the call will go badly, but I know that now is the time.

He picks up on the first ring. Call display tells him it's me. He's still angry, anger edging through every word, but I have the feeling that now there's something else. He doesn't want to give up, still wants revenge on his former employers. My idea about him, at this moment, is that he doesn't want to waste his anger on me, doesn't want to waste a drop of it, still, if possible, wants to use me as a weapon against them. He wants to use me and then throw me away. Nothing he says particularly indicates this, it is simply what I've come to understand about Emmett. I don't know if he was always like this. I think back to the way he first explained it to me, the way he told his own story, that from the moment he was fired he's been whittling himself away, carving himself into a self-made shiv of bitterness. That is what I now think I hear in his voice. He is a person who uses people and then throws them away. As I explain, I realize that I also want to use him, don't care what happens to him after.

It takes an extremely long time to explain: where I am, what I'm trying to do, what I want from him. He is listening to me but at the same time not listening, which is why I must explain slowly, repeating key details several times. Gradually he starts to get it, and I can feel him turning the question over in his mind: how might my suggestion constitute revenge? He wants revenge, something ugly, something vicious, and what I'm proposing seems somehow too noble to fit the bill. He's trying not to turn his anger on me, keep it focused on the real enemy. At least now he knows what we want, which makes me feel that the worst of this call is over. As he continues to question me I'm almost sure it won't work. It's like I've painted him into a corner, and he's used to being in charge, hates being painted into a corner or simply prefers to do so himself. I've presented him with a plan he doesn't like, is anathema to his character and values, but it seems he doesn't have a better plan he can get behind instead. My shitty plan might be the only one he's got, his only shot at revenge. I can feel that he hates not having other options, that it almost makes him sick. After a long pause he seems distracted, changes the topic.
—You want to hear something strange?

—All right.
—Our rich friend thinks I hired you to strangle him with a piano wire.
—How do you know that?
—He hired a detective to track you down. The detective is a friend of mine. Told me the whole story.

I didn't know what to say. I didn't want to admit what I was feeling, but my pride was hurt. The plan to strangle the billionaire was my plan. I didn't want to share it with Emmett. I didn't want Emmett to take all the credit for a plan that had taken up years of my life. It didn't matter if the plot had failed, it was mine and I didn't want him to have it. He interrupted my thoughts, my self-pity.
—You didn't manage to kill him, but you certainly made him paranoid.
—What do you mean?
—I'm still having him followed. Not all the time. Just the highlights. He's lost his touch. It's not like before. I don't know what's changed exactly. Not everything goes his way.
—I did that?
—I don't know. Maybe he's just getting old.

I thought I had done nothing and now here was Emmett, this bitter, angry, disembodied voice on the other end of the line, offering me a glimmer of hope. I had a thought, a spark, that every failure contains at least a seed of something else, even if there's no way of knowing precisely what. When he spoke again he seemed even more lost in thought, somewhere off by himself in the middle of nowhere.
—I'm remembering something I read once about Roosevelt.
—Why are you telling me about Roosevelt?
—Don't interrupt me.

—What did you read?

—That he was a class traitor. That he was a traitor to his own class. And they hated him for it.

I was making the call from a toilet stall at the library. It was the first place I could think of that was quiet and private. There was banging on the stall and, thinking someone wanted to use it, I stood up and opened the door. I was not expecting to see three large men with masks but knew exactly who they were. Suddenly, without thinking, I started screaming as loudly as I could. Just screaming. A long, loud endless sound coming from somewhere in my body, I didn't know where. As I screamed the men began punching and kicking me. Also as I screamed I could hear Emmett on the other end of the line, swearing a blue streak, asking what the fuck was going on. I keeled over in the stall, continued to scream, as they dragged me out into the middle of the floor. Just then the door to the washroom opened and two elderly women peered in. I couldn't get a good look at them from down on the floor but assumed they were the librarians. A heel came down hard and fast on my cell phone, smashing it to bits, crushing my hand in the process, Emmett's voice yelling "someone tell me what the fuck is going on" smashed into bits as well. I had a feeling I would never hear that voice again as I continued to scream and the three men momentarily stopped kicking me and stared at the two older women. It was the strangest kind of standoff I could ever imagine, the two librarians wondering what their favourite pianist could have possibly done to invite such a beating, the men wondering if they should attack the women, or if attacking old women was where they drew the line. I keep screaming, and to my utter surprise, to everyone's surprise, the two librarians start screaming as well, all three of us screaming in unison, I'm tempted to say in harmony. I'm surprised I have so much air in my lungs and have no idea how the two librarians keep up right along with me. Then some others come up behind them—a few people in the library, drawn towards the commotion, which is strange because the library is so often empty—and the three masks decide to cut their losses and push their way out. As they're pushing through the librarians, one of them glances back at me, meets my now-watering eyes. I can see his eyes through the slots in his mask, and his look tells me that as far as he's concerned I'm already dead. It's only a matter of time.

1.

I arrive in Singapore and there's no one at the airport to pick me up. This has never happened before. I scan the arrivals hall over and over again, searching for the telltale sign with my name on it, but it is nowhere to be found. I sit down in the generic airport café and order an espresso, even though it's midnight here, then pull out the brief and start leafing through it. At the top of the last page, in bold and underlined, is the sentence: "No one will pick you up at the airport. Take a limousine," followed by the address of the hotel. There is no explanation as to why no one is here to pick me up, only the benign understatement of this unprecedented occurrence, as if it were an unremarkable fact. (Though, in a sense, the bold and underlining does partially serve to remark upon it.) I get in a limousine, check into the hotel, and lie awake all night getting angrier and angrier that no one was waiting for me when I arrived.

The next day there is someone to pick me up at the hotel and drive me to the meeting. However, as we drive it takes me more than a few minutes to understand what he's explaining to me. That he's the head of the division, and decided to pick me up himself because every single person working for him is currently on strike. There was also a slight fear that if he entrusted it to an employee I might be kidnapped, since the strikers were currently activating every last scrap of leverage they could lay their hands on. Finally, it was his pleasure to meet me in person and be my driver for the day. I realize this situation is the reason I was handed such a lengthy brief on labour unrest in preparation for the trip. I clearly should have read everything more carefully, but my general tendency for these meetings is to improvise, to skim the brief and then see what happens. Since they are more or less only fact-finding missions, and nothing concrete has to be negotiated or decided, I see no harm heading in guerrilla-style and then making the best of whatever happens next. As we drive he explains to me that now, as the strike is heading into its seventh month, they have finally run out of back inventory and will soon be forced to settle. He looks to me almost for sympathy, as he insists that they absolutely held out for as long as they could, going on to explain that in the negotiations to come they will make as few concessions as possible.

We pull up in front of the largest, densest picket line I have seen in my life. There must be thousands of them. We can't actually go into the offices, he continues to explain, but he simply wanted to make sure I saw this for myself. We both stare out the front window of the car at the waves and waves of people surrounding the building. We sit there for a while before they all start to chant in perfect unison. My companion explains that they're chanting that if they all stand together nothing can stop them, nothing can stop them and they will win. We listen for a while and then go for lunch.

Over lunch there is so much he wants to explain, as if I had the power to grant him capitalist absolution, and if he explains it all in enough detail I will eventually do so. He explains that of the thousands of people we just saw picketing, only a fraction actually work for his division. Somehow the strike has generalized, become a more general protest against business and against conventional society. By showing their solidarity with the workers, people from all walks of life can have the feeling they've become part of a fight they can actually win. He then corrects himself, he had just said all walks of life, and perhaps some of them had been in all walks of life before they lost their jobs, but now they were mostly unemployed. His worst fear at the moment is that the protesters will find a way to occupy the building, get rid of management, and run the division as a workers co-op. There is much talk these days of taking over businesses in this way and therefore, somehow, changing capitalism from within. Like some had already managed to do in Argentina. He is sure there are many on the picket line, maybe thousands, who would love to see his business used as a test case, the first domino to topple so to speak. A few years ago the government would have simply rolled in and arrested everyone, but there's a new government now, elected on a platform of change, and they don't like the optics of using their first year in office to break the longest and most popular strike in recent history. They want us to negotiate, he says, and soon we'll have no choice.

What he couldn't understand, what he was still trying to work out, is how the workers managed to win over such a massive display of popular support, to win over the masses and make him into the villain. Because there was no question in his mind that, in the current popular imagination he was a worse villain, more evil, than any screenwriter was capable of dreaming up. I wondered if this was pure paranoia on his part or if there was any truth to the public relations nightmare he was describing at such great length. He wondered if the best thing to do was to resign, let someone else engage in the long, painful negotiation that would hopefully end the strike without ending the profitability of the division. Maybe there was someone that wanted his job who at the same time also had the ability to sell him- or herself—for a moment I thought he had said 'scam' him- or herself—as a friend to the workers. His own reputation, in this sense, was now so poor he feared it would only be a liability. He had always, in his long and successful career, done everything he could to maximize value for his shareholders, and he didn't see how this simple, practical fact could now be held up as an evil greater than biblical sin. But in the court of popular opinion, that was where things stood. He then said he had two questions for me: 1) did I come here to close down the division and 2) if not, or even if this was the case, what did I think of the situation and what did I think he should do?

I consider the matter for a long time before answering, perhaps too long, because when I finally look at him, really look at him, he seems anxious to the point of terror. I realize he thinks I'm the wrecking crew, here to destroy him and his career. But I'm not the wrecking crew, and when I finally do speak I try to explain some thoughts I'd had on the plane, about the zeitgeist, how this particular strike should not be viewed in isolation, but as one sharp yet slight aspect of a much larger cultural moment. I can tell this isn't what he wants to hear. He sees himself only as the victim, a casualty of this particular zeitgeist, does not see any opportunity in it. I try explaining that every setback must also be viewed as potential, that he must put these questions in perspective, but basically he isn't listening, or all he hears is the fact that I don't have a magic bullet up my sleeve, am not actually here to help or rescue him. He offers to drive me back to my hotel. If I want, he says, we can go watch the strike for a while longer. He says he has watched it every day from a safe distance, sitting in his car. He watches every day, wondering what exactly it is they want, what exactly he should do to resolve the situation without losing face. He's getting more and more worried about himself, about how each day he drives to his former workplace and spends an hour, or several hours, watching the crowd surround the building. He's worried he's starting to find it beautiful.

2.

At the hospital they bandage up my hand. Since moving to the field I had kept what was left of my life savings strapped to my thigh. I use about a quarter of this money to pay the hospital. Of course I haven't been the only one beaten. Over the next days I learn they've tracked down as many workers as they could find. The attacks are always the same: they find workers out alone, far away from the field, and beat us within an inch of our life. It is obvious why they don't want to come for us in the field, where they would have to face thousands of angry workers all at the same time. At the next meeting we decide to only travel in packs, don't go anywhere in a group of less than ten. We're starting to put together a strategy. Different subcontractors run different buses and different crops; they don't all work together, at least not yet, so it will be hard for them to present a united front. We are sure there must be some way we can use this chaos, this lack of coordination, to our advantage.

There was a particular moment I will always remember from

that last decisive meeting before the strike. The mentor had brought a giant chalkboard out into the field. Where she got such a chalkboard, or why she thought it was necessary, are both aspects of this moment I am unable to unravel, but it took four of us to carry it from the roof of her car out towards the bonfire. On the chalkboard she had made lists of all the tasks that needed to be done, and as she read these tasks, people called out their names to volunteer. Very quickly the chalkboard filled with names and each name called out seemed to me like one step closer to the oncoming storm. I had unstrapped my life savings from my thigh and decided to spend the rest of it on food and water for the strike. If the strike was successful I would find other ways to survive, and if it failed I would be dead, in jail or expelled from the country. In at least two of these scenarios I would have little need for cash.

When the chalkboard was full, the mentor asked us all to sit for a minute of silence. The silence was for her husband, who had died in a struggle much like the one we planned to start first thing tomorrow. But it was also for every worker who had ever suffered or died in a struggle for their basic rights. We all sat in silence, nothing to listen to but the crackle of fire, and during the silence I thought about all these people I had met since coming here. How they had accepted me almost immediately, laughed at and with me, taken my foolhardy plan—was it a plan or was it only a desire—almost more seriously than I had at first. I then wondered if any of the men sitting with us were spies, rats on the payroll of one of the subcontractors, and the minute this meeting was over they would run to the bosses and describe anything and everything they could remember. But a minute of commemorative silence is not the right time to be thinking of rats, and before it was done I hope I gave at least a few seconds for a quick prayer that we'd all survive, that whatever happens next we don't turn on each other and instead find ways to lend each other our strength. She must have been reading my mind, because the mentor brought the silence to a close by asking each of us to look inside ourselves. (I wanted to roll my eyes but also didn't want to undermine her in any way.) She said we each should think long and hard to figure out where we, each of us individually, could find the strength to hold out, to keep going for as long as it takes.

She then thought we should each say something, a few words or a few sentences. These words could be anything, but if we all listened to each other, we could later remember what others had said in moments we were losing faith or the will to go on. What each of us said now might be like a message in a bottle we were throwing into the future, to lend us hope at some future moment we might need it the most. Once again, after each of us had said his piece, there were quiet pockets of translation. Statement, translation, statement, translation, and on it went until every last one of us had said at least a few words. I learned so much as we went round and around. It was both heartfelt and heartbreaking. I don't think I've ever listened that hard in my life. I wish I could now remember every last word, but I don't, so I fear these are just a few of the lines I still recall, that stuck with me, though I'm sure I've gotten some of them slightly wrong, and perhaps with others completely missed the point.

"If I ever have children I don't want their life like this. Or when any of us have children. Our children should have something else."

"Make the bastards pay."

"Dignity. That is what makes life worth living. We all know this."

"I came here looking for a better life and all we get is shit. And yet today I feel something different."

"I look around at all the faces and think: these are the people I want to fight with. Win or lose, I feel proud to be doing this with all of you."

"We have no choice. We win or we die."

"If my father could see me now, I know he would be proud of me."

"Those fuckers will learn to treat us with respect."

"I'm afraid. There's no shame in admitting you're afraid. But I won't back down."

"When I think that we're all in this together, it almost makes me want to cry."

"Dignity. I also think that's the best word. Dignity."

"They beat us but they don't yet kill us. They think if they beat a few dozen of us we'll get scared and back down. That's maybe what always happened before. They beat a few of the troublemakers and everyone else backed down. But now we're organized and it will take more than a few beatings to stop us."

"I just want to stand up. I just want to look the problem in the eyes and stay on my feet."

"If we fight, whatever else happens, they no longer own us like they did before. Already there's something we've won."

"We aren't slaves. No one should ever be able to say that they own us."

"I can't fucking wait to tell them about this back home."

"Just a few weeks ago all of this seemed impossible to me. I still can barely believe any of this is happening. It's like a dream."

"I can feel it in my bones. We're going to win. Maybe not everything, but we're going to win."

"Some day all these fields will be workers' co-ops. And the capitalists will no longer get a share."

1.

I was told it would be an informal gathering. Instead it feels more like a job review. But it was only an informal gathering. And, after all, who were they to review me. I sit at the front of the boardroom, doing my best to ooze my natural charm, to speak to each of the colleagues staring at me as if I was speaking to them alone. The order of my talk is easy enough to achieve, each of the places I've visited and what I may or may not have learned there: Cologne, Milan, Zurich, Singapore, etc. But as I'm placing my spin across each of these stories, I can feel the spin is not quite taking shape. As I'm talking—I don't know why I didn't notice this before—I realize each of these stories is almost only about me, has little to do with the relative health or strength of the organization. I don't know if others in the room are picking up on it, but as the cities I visited pile up in my recounting of them, I feel I am recounting yet another cliché of a cliché: the man who travelled the world only to find himself dissecting the minutiae of his own reflection.

As I am talking I'm also trying to shift tactics, wondering if there's some tentative way to float out my new idea—CEO as supportive friend to the worker—to see if I can bring the idea into the room in a manner that doesn't incite panic. I decide I'll try to do so within the shell of the story of the Italian kid. How the new young workers consider themselves virtuosos, and perhaps there is a new kind of virtuosity for our organization to engage in. A virtuosity in making our workers feel valued and supported. Even before this sentence is entirely out of my mouth I feel I am in the process of making one of the worst missteps in my entire career. It's like I've said we're going to make money by spreading the plague. (Actually, if I had said that, I believe the reaction would have been considerably more positive.) But I've always been a visionary, and sometimes being a visionary means pushing past negative reactions to the success that lies on the other side. The more you gamble the more you win, if you win. But, of course, also the more you lose. How big a gamble was this and was it one I could actually win? Was this informal gathering the right place to be making my tentative first move? I look around the room and have another thought, also extremely obvious. These are all men who dream of some day having my job, of taking me out and taking my spot. This isn't paranoia or is it? When I was their age, if I had found myself in a similar situation, I would have certainly wanted to do the same.

After the meeting is over I can't stop thinking about it. It's like

I've already made the first move in a chess game that might last for the rest of my natural life and worry that my opening gambit was extremely poor. But I'm still in charge. I can still choose to pack up the pieces and put away the board, go back to whatever game I was playing before (not chess but perhaps Monopoly). Never before have I shied away from a challenge, why would I start now? But is this the challenge I want? How do you know what you do or don't want before it's too late to turn back? I'm trying to step back from myself, look at the situation as I would if it concerned someone else. An aging CEO—always known for his panache, shrewdness and rapacity—decides to turn over a new leaf for the final chapter of his life and make life better for some actual people. Does it sound like something noble or does it sound like complete bullshit? Why is there no one close by who I trust enough to fully discuss these matters?

I'm thinking back to the informal gathering, how I couldn't manage to get on top of it, couldn't find a way to fully dominate the room, something I believe I once managed to do effortlessly. So if I can no longer dominate maybe there's some other way, instead of domination something more like co-operation or collaboration. An organization that people work for because they want to be there, and a slightly decreased margin of profit is in fact a small price to pay for the energy I will get in doing the right thing. You catch more flies with honey than you do with poison, and yet I know the opposite is also true: if you give people a few small benefits and concessions, they will keep demanding more and more, practically forever. Try to be a friend to the workers and they will treat you like a cash machine that dispenses free cash until your dying day. And yet there still must be some way to get away with murder, to have the best of both worlds, to have our employees see me as a hero while I remain in control, never letting them feel they have the upper hand. This is the magic trick I will need to master if I only want to lose a few pawns without ever sacrificing the king. What kind of king is loved by his subjects and is it too late for me to make a play for such populist love?

For weeks and weeks I think about my presentation, which for all intents and purposes went normally enough, but it keeps coming back into my thoughts like an ongoing curse: what have I begun and what have I done. And yet, at the same time, I'm still not sure it's actually started. I'm still not sure I've done anything at all.

2.

Sitting in the library these past few weeks, reading about the history of labour, I have often been shocked by the ferocity of violence directed against the workers. I remember something I heard as a child; I feel almost certain it came from my parents: if at the very beginning you knew how hard it would be you'd simply never start. Tomorrow we start, and though I now know so much more then when I first arrived, I still have basically no idea how it will be. How long a fight we're actually in for. All I know is that, however naively, it has already begun and there's no turning back. I know I need to sleep but I'm too wired, lying awake in this tent: thinking, thinking, thinking.

I have never felt so energized, so alive, so frightened, so engaged and supported. But this is only the beginning—when we're still gaining energy, when everything feels possible—and later, as the strike progresses, everything will only become more difficult. Tomorrow will be perhaps the most challenging day of my entire life and I now realize I will have to face it with relatively little sleep. All of the reading I have done in the library in some way tells the same story over and over again: that they will do practically anything to protect exorbitant profits, resort to any savagery or brutality, but with guile and perseverance it is possible to wear them down, to win concessions. I know I shouldn't be asking myself these questions now, that I should be steeling myself for the upcoming battle, but I can't help but wonder: are concessions really enough? Around the bonfire someone said we must turn all these fields into co-ops, and that might be another step in the right direction, but would even that be enough? There is so much injustice in the world, the more you know the more endless it seems. So much of this injustice is aimed at people who look more or less like me, who come from parts of the world far from the so-called centre, but why do they only take from us? Why must we take all the bullets? They want our labour, for as cheap as possible, and they want our resources, and it's easier to take from those you can say are different, from those you assume are less, even if you're no longer able to say so as blatantly as they once did. And then hatred always has the fire to take on a life of its own. Concessions aren't nearly enough, but this is where I've landed and this is what I will fight for in the long days to come.

If we make a union in these fields, is there anything we can do to ensure it doesn't become corrupt? Or that later it doesn't only look after the people who work here, we just look after our own, and everyone else can fend for themselves? We need to fight for ourselves, here and now, but we also need changes so large and impossible they encompass the entire world. I wonder if things moved so fast here because we could sit in a circle and talk, look each other in the eyes, feel each other's presence, that we had each other's backs, and I have no idea how that could ever happen on a global scale. I'm wondering how much I've really changed since the piano wire in my jacket pocket felt like my only hope. Or how much more I might change in the future. Here in the fields, since I got here and this terrifying project began, I've had such an intense feeling of people coming together, that people here want to care for each other, that this wanting to care for each other is so much more important than any money or benefits we might eventually be able to wring from the organization. How can we keep wanting to care for each other, not turn on each other, as things continue to get more difficult.

That we have to care for each other, that must be the point. Right now we must fight, as hard and for long as it takes, but we can't just keep fighting forever. Sooner or later we will have to stop fighting and care for each other. This is actually the real work. To be with people who we care for, and who care for us, instead of working for people who care nothing for our well-being. The more I think, the less likely it seems I will fall asleep any time soon. I'm full of doubts but know I cannot let these doubts stop me. There is so much in life we have absolutely no control of. My parents weren't religious, or politics was their religion, and I've never considered believing in any church or any god, but I can see how at a moment like this, how useful it would be to believe in something, to have some otherworldly faith. So many times around the bonfire I heard the word dignity, that we want to live with dignity, and I wonder if this desire for dignity might be a kind of faith. A faith that there's some basic value to being alive and that we all partake in this value. If you look around, people are being killed all the time, left to die, left to their own devices without resources to survive, for no good reason, and I don't know how we can say that all these deaths, all these lives, were lived with dignity. I want to think that when we start fighting tomorrow we are also fighting for all of them, but worry we are only fighting for ourselves.

Sitting in the library I read about so many unions that began as bold, noble fights and over time declined into complacency, corruption or even worse. Imperialist unions that supported the destruction of left-wing unions in other countries. A story that repeats over and over again. Today I know we are not corrupt; we are fighting for our lives and all our reasons are good. But what can we possibly do about the future? Christ preached love and then the inquisition was a rolling orgy of hatred committed in his name. How do so many things devolve into their opposite over time? I keep telling myself that now is not the time to worry about such things. Now is the time to focus on the possibilities for our immediate struggle. And, at the same time, it is always the time to question oneself and one's motives, if only to sharpen the blade, to make sure one's blind spots don't hide monsters that in the long run might upset the entire game.

I remember reading an interview with a concert pianist, perhaps one of the most successful musicians of his generation, who had much of his success when he was very young, just starting out. The interviewer asked him what it was like to be so successful so young, and his reply always stuck with me. He said there was so much happening, so much coming at him all at the same time, that he barely even experienced it happening, barely had a moment to take it in or enjoy. In the weeks or months or even years to come I feel my life will be the same, overwhelming. I will be overwhelmed by all the obstacles, tensions and decisions that must be made. But as I lie here in this tent unable to sleep, I tell myself I must pay attention, I must experience everything that is about to happen to me as fully as possible, I must experience it as some kind of joy. I can't just let it all speed by without living it fully. I can't let this life or struggle happen without me. But it is possible that it might, that it all will blur past and when it's over I'll look back and barely know what happened. Either way I will live with the results.

I don't know at what time I finally drifted off, or how long I managed to sleep, but it couldn't have been for long, and either before I drifted off, or shortly thereafter, I could already feel dawn cracking through the edges of the cheap tent. Even in the tumult of my anticipations and doubts, the morning light was here to tell me that it has all already begun.

1.

Emmett phoned me. It was the first time I had heard his voice in I don't know how many years. The moment he started talking I had the devastating feeling that he wants something. He's not just calling to chat. Later I had to ask myself: why did I find this feeling so devastating. I had to admit that all this time I'd harboured a secret hope that some day Emmett would call to offer the olive branch, would call for no other reason than to rekindle our friendship. But this was not such a call. As he is talking, trying to explain something to me, I feel distracted, trying to listen to this Emmett on the other end of the line while at the same time remembering the Emmett from before, the old Emmett, the Emmett I used to know. I find myself trying to remember the last time we spoke and what was actually said. Trying to remember if that final conversation began with me calling him or him calling me.

I remember him saying that he hoped I burned in hell, my reply that I knew he didn't mean it and his insistence that he did. He told me that he had dedicated his life to me, that I didn't know what a friend was or how to be one, and that I now had to spend the rest of my life watching my back because some day he would get his revenge, served cold as ice. When he had saved my job, saved my company, he had done so on the assumption that we were in this together, that we had each other's backs until the very end, and he would have done things very differently if he had known that I in fact saw his back as little more than a target. As he said all this I remember the way I sat hunched in my chair, in my office, trying to think of some way to de-escalate the situation, to bring him back towards me, but any word I spoke just poured gasoline on his fury. I understood his position but still felt there was some way for us to work it out. He promised he would hurt me, that whatever I'd just done to him he would someday do to me but one hundred thousand times worse. He said that I wasn't a human being, and that every time I looked in the mirror I should remember that my best friend in the world now doesn't even think I'm human and wishes nothing more than I burn in the most disgusting of hells for all eternity. Then he hung up and that was the last time I heard his voice until today.

His tone today is almost the opposite, more calm than calm, so calm it's almost deadening. He's telling me about a situation he feels I should be aware of, that he thinks I should see for myself. He keeps repeating the day and time, saying that I should be there. That it is an important event that would be made even more important by my presence. He is speaking as if I already know what he's talking about and somehow I am ashamed to admit that I don't. He explains that he hasn't contacted me in so long, and I should take the fact that he is contacting me now as evidence that this is a call towards something that truly matters. He then changes the subject, telling me he knows I am in crisis, not explaining how he knows, but that it's all right since he's in crisis as well. He knows that his crisis is because of me but is not yet certain if my crisis is because of him. So much time has passed but he feels convinced that he still knows me better than anyone. Don't I know you better than anyone, he asks, and I am forced to admit that he probably does.

I have never heard him so calm, so melancholy, so focused. Because he knows me so well he is sure that if I show up at the date and time he specifies, the date, time and place he repeats over and over again, it will be an important moment, both for me and the organization. It might not be a lesson I like but it will definitely teach me something important, something I need to know. I think about following his instructions and it feels like walking into a trap. I can tell that Emmett already knows this set-up sounds like a trap, perhaps that is why he has made his voice so calm. But the old Emmett confidence is still in full effect and therefore he also believes I will simply be persuaded by the pure force of his argument and comply. As I'm listening I am gripped by a feeling that I don't remember ever having in my life. It is so uncanny, and many times when I later think back on it, even then I feel completely drained. The feeling is so simple I don't even know if it has a name. I want to ask him to forgive me. But I don't, and I don't think in the few short sentences I have uttered during our brief conversation I let my voice crack even once. He doesn't get the upper hand. I curtly say I will research and consider his proposal and then hang up. In the silence that follows, I wonder if I will ever hear his voice again.

2.

The buses roll up but no one gets on. Not a single worker. We all stand in the dust and don't get on. That is how it starts. Instead of getting on the buses, as we have always done, we just stand there staring at them, staring them down, our arms linked as we surround them. Already, as the buses are pulling in, I am startled to see how many television cameras have arrived. I had underestimated Emmett, he really came through: I said get us media attention and here it is. I am trying to count them but it's difficult in all the early tangle and commotion. There must be at least a dozen television crews here, all angling for the best possible shot. Already things are going better than I possibly imagined. As we stand in stoic silence, the buses unable to move forward or back as we surround them, I am imagining what it will look like on television, an image of quiet strength and solidarity. The subcontractors knew this strike was coming, but it seems they weren't expecting it this soon, because the police and scabs haven't arrived yet. Dawn is still breaking and there is no one here but us, the bus drivers and television crews. I can't quite explain it, everything is such a strange mix of stillness and commotion.

When the police arrive the mood changes quickly. Police vans start pulling up and keep pulling up for hours. It is as if they've already decided to outnumber us and can of course do so effortlessly. In two hours the entire field is surrounded and they're on their megaphones repeating over and over again that this strike is illegal, we must disperse immediately, this strike is illegal, we must get on the buses, get back to work, this strike is illegal, through the tepid buzz of the megaphones, over and over again for hours. We stand our ground, keep the buses from moving, and the cops also hold their ground, surrounding us with their numbing megaphone repetitions. We eat lunch all still standing, surrounding the buses that have now been abandoned by their drivers, and in late afternoon the scabs start to arrive. It's strange to me that at first there aren't that many, maybe a hundred or so, as they fan out across the field in packs of five or ten, unclear what precisely they are there to do, sizing up the situation in a manner that might almost be described as relaxed, nonetheless making us nervous, sniffing around towards their first move if we don't make our move first. A few try to get between us and the buses but we don't let them and they don't yet insist. Everything is still calm, but tensions can't help but gradually creep forward, and I scan the field nervously waiting for something to crack.

I don't know what time it is when the first rock is thrown, nor am I quick enough to catch who threw it. Later, several witnesses claim it was thrown by one of the scabs, thrown directly into the face of a cop who had momentarily let his shield down in boredom, but of course the newspapers will say it was thrown by one of us. One rock is all it takes for the cops to storm in. Suddenly I am in the middle and no overview is possible. I'm being pushed and pulled from every direction. Out of the corner of my eye I see a scab charging a police officer, see him smashed towards the ground, blood from his head mixing into the dust. As the violence is starting I already feel I'm in some strange sort of theatre. All those actually fighting work for the bosses, some of them pretending to be workers while others pretend to be police. Actors fighting as if the cameras were rolling and they are. I realize this is what will actually be on the news tonight, violent foreign workers attacking noble white cops. But this is only the beginning and maybe the story will still change over time. A fist hits my head, I don't see where it came from or who it belongs to. I immediately feel dizzy, wonder if one punch is all it takes, if I'm going down, will be trampled to death by the people I love most, but manage to regain my balance, slide through the bodies and I'm standing again. The drivers have made it back into their buses and are pulling away as so many of us continue to mob around in an attempt to stop them, the cops beating us down or dragging us away. It is only later I learn that we managed to get into the engines, someone knew which part to remove, that many of the buses broke down less than a mile from this field. When they write about today, years from now, it's something every story will mention, how we managed to stop the buses: first one way, then another.

Cops are handcuffing workers and dragging them into the vans at the edge of the field. I see the mentor at the far end, handcuffed and shoved into a vehicle, doing her best to shove back. If we actually succeed, I realize at that moment, it will be because of her. A few feet in front of me two cops are handcuffing a man they've slammed down onto his knees as I rush forward to intervene, pushing one cop out of the way as my friend pulls free and runs. The other night around the fire he was the first one to use the word dignity. In a second two guns are pressed against either side of my head and my hands are high in the air in surrender. Time is completely detached from itself; I can barely follow the words they are yelling at me, barely separate them from the dull buzz of the megaphone: this strike is illegal, you must disperse immediately, this strike is illegal, etc. I think: I am finally doing it. What I was always told is impossible. I am dying for a cause. It was probably on a day much like today that my parents were killed. I always thought they had died for nothing, but suddenly now realize almost the opposite is true. I have judged them wanting and was completely and utterly wrong. I feel both cops about to pull the trigger, that in a moment I'll be dead, and open my mouth to scream but can't understand what's happening, I'm not screaming but singing, I'm singing as loud as I possibly can, one of the old songs I've been figuring out in the library. Some memory from my previous life already knows it's the most popular one, the song we all know. The cops on either side of me are so surprised that they pause, probably only for a few moments, but it seems long enough for those around me to start singing as well. They all know the song but we're each singing it in our own language, with slightly different words, a song that spreads like a wildfire. It's the strangest thing. All the workers are singing but the scabs don't know the melody or the words. In less than a moment it becomes violently clear who is one of us and who is one of them. We are all singing at the top of our lungs. I have never heard so many sing so loudly. There is still fighting but it is as if the singing has taken over. The cops are handcuffing us and dragging us towards the vans as we continue to sing. There are still two guns against my head but, as I continue to sing at the top of my lungs, I'm not as sure as I was before that they're actually going to fire. My arms are raised high above my head in surrender. As I continue to sing I feel a secret hope that on television tomorrow there will be fighting but there will also be singing. That as we continue to sing this song that we all heard as children, as we continue to sing the world will actually hear us, that they will see us and hear us on their screens.

I am singing at the top of my lungs, looking straight ahead, and at the far end of the field I see an armoured SUV pull up. It is like there is a voice in my head that tells me: keep singing as loud as you can and keep staring at the SUV. I watch body-guards get out of the car with their guns drawn, and behind the bodyguards I see him, the man I had tried to strangle with the piano wire, stepping out of the vehicle, taking a moment to adjust, taking in the scene. I don't know what he's doing here but then suddenly think that I do. Emmett sent him. I start walking toward the SUV, one careful step at a time, sure that the cops will shoot me with each and every step, and I don't know why, perhaps because I'm singing, perhaps because we're all singing so loudly as if we are all one voice, but the cops don't shoot, instead walk alongside me, their guns still pointed at my head. It takes only a few steps before our eyes meet. I am staring straight at the billionaire, we make eye contact, and I can see that he recognizes me. I can see that he recognizes me, that he hears me, hears all of us. And I can tell that, as he recognizes me, he is shaken.